THE GOOD TEACHER

A GRIPPING DOMESTIC THRILLER

EMILY SHINER

GREY

"Half-caff ice vanilla latte with sweet cream cold foam?" The barista holds up my drink and I have to shoulder my way through the crowd to get to the counter. When I reach for my drink, I feel his gaze fall on me and his eyebrows fly up in amazement. "This is yours, sir?"

The surprise in his voice is evident and I nod, taking it from him. "Yep, it's mine," I confirm, my mouth already watering in anticipation.

All around me there's so much movement and noise that I know the only way I'm going to enjoy my drink in peace is if I get out of here, so I turn and push my way back through the crowd, exhaling as I leave the hustle and bustle of the café behind me.

I have to admit, when this old building on Main Street was sold and we heard that a hip new coffee place called Cool Beans would be going in, I was skeptical. For my entire adult life I'd lived off of nothing but black drip coffee and made it this far in my career without any problems, but one taste of this sweet concoction and I was sold.

The only problem is that they don't have a dedicated parking lot, which means that the morning rush of people trying to get their coffee fix before heading in to start work can almost completely shut down Main Street. I nimbly dodge a mother with a crying child and look both ways before darting across the street.

Luckily for me, the hospital is just two blocks away. I can stretch my legs and mentally prepare for the day while drinking my coffee without anyone bothering me. My steps eat up the sidewalk and I barely look around at my surroundings as I walk.

This morning I have an ablation planned on a young girl. She's just sixteen, far too young to be dealing with tachycardia, but I'm confident that I can fix her. After lunch I'm putting a stent into an older man. At our last appointment he was telling me about how he's finally a grandfather after years of waiting. The fact that he wanted nothing more than to live long enough to see his grandchildren grow up touched me.

I'd like to think he's in the best hands.

"Dr. Bennett!" A loud voice cuts over the noise of the hospital parking lot and I pause, turning to look at the doctor walking over to meet me. Dr. Cherry Davies has long red hair that matches her name, a pert little nose, and a smile so big that all of the patients in the ER suddenly forget that their lives are in a shambles if she's in the room.

She greets me and plucks the coffee from my hand, taking an experimental sip and then immediately wrinkling her nose. "That," she says, handing my cup back to me, "is a crime against humanity. Are you sure that it's even legal for them to be in business selling an abomination like that and calling it coffee?"

"It is sweet," I agree, enjoying another sip. "But I love it."

"Because you've been a bachelor for too long. Remind me again why you aren't dating?" She falls into place next to me and the two of us walk up to the hospital entrance together. Most people who didn't know Cherry well would think that she was flirting with me, but I know better.

On the day that I met her, she told me that she was in a long-term monogamous relationship with her cat Felix and no man could ever compare. I've offered to set her up on dates before, but she's just laughed at me and asked me if I really knew a man who could keep up.

She's right. When she's not saving lives in the ER she's busy hang gliding or traveling halfway across the world to try some cuisine she saw on the travel channel. She might look like she would be snapped up in a moment by any eligible bachelor, but the truth is I don't know a single person who could keep pace with her without having a heart attack.

"I don't date," I tell her, "for the same reason that you don't."

This makes her laugh and she grabs the large handle of the front door, pulling it open and gesturing me through. "You don't date because there isn't anyone in this world crazy enough to put up with you?"

I grin. "Something like that." The antiseptic smell of the hospital always assaults my nostrils when it first hits me every day, but that's how you can tell that everything is clean and ready to go. Our hospital may be small, but we have wonderful stats of keeping people alive and making sure that they make it home to their loved ones.

I feel as if I have the best of both worlds. Working in a small mountain hospital means all of the fun of a larger city without the stress. I love it here, but I didn't move here just for my mental health.

"I know, I know, you have to make sure that you choose the right person for Lilah," she says, and I nod. "I get that. You're a good dad, Grey...no matter what people say about you." She grins again and smacks me playfully on the arm before turning in the direction of the ER and announcing her arrival. "I'm here to save lives and chew bubble gum and I'm all out of bubble gum!"

Her ensuing laughter is cut off when the double doors to the ER slam shut behind her. Turning, I shake my head, then drain my coffee on the way to my office. Cherry is a hot mess, that's for sure, but she makes working here fun. Most of the doctors here are on good terms, and I know that some of them go out for drinks once in a while.

If I didn't need to go straight home to Lilah, I might consider that, but my daughter takes and always will take top priority. Sitting behind my desk, I pick up a framed picture and lightly touch it with my finger. It's hard to look at a photo of my dead wife every single day, but I don't ever want to forget what she looked like.

The older Lilah gets, the more she looks like Sara. They have the same soft brown eyes and blonde hair. Lilah likes to sniff bites of new food before trying them just like her mother did. When she laughs and I'm not looking at her, the sound, I'd swear that her mother was still alive.

My stomach turns and I set the picture back down on my desk. I'll always miss her, no matter how long she's been gone.

Six years later, and I still want her here with me. We had no idea that she was sick until the ovarian cancer was so advanced that all we could do was keep her comfortable at the end. I still regret it: regret not pushing her harder for more or better treatments, regret not trying everything in my power to keep her alive.

But she was ready and didn't want her last few months to be lost to the drugs. She wanted to enjoy Lilah. Our daughter is fifteen now and I wish more than anything that she had her mother back. The best I can do is promise her is that I'll keep her safe. I'll keep anything bad from ever happening to her.

LILAH

*I*t's Friday night, and where am I?

Not at Trevor's party, which he promised was going to be the best end to the school year ever.

Not out getting pizza with my friends who are apparently too cool to go out to a party.

Nope. I'm on the sofa, eating a frozen burrito that I didn't microwave enough, so the inside is still a little cold, watching a documentary on a serial killer. My dad would probably have a hernia if he knew what I was watching, but hey, he's not here.

What can I say, I love my friends, but I'm a bit of a homebody.

My phone vibrates but I ignore it, instead forcing myself to take another bite of the undernuked burrito. Dad was supposed to be home tonight but apparently there was an emergency surgery that he had to go in for. It's great that he works so hard, and everyone in town knows and likes him for that, but sometimes I just wish that he were here with me more.

My phone vibrates again and I roll my eyes, grabbing it

from the armrest and clicking on the screen. It's so dark in the living room that the bright light from the screen makes me shield my eyes while I read the message.

On my way home! Need anything?

As I stare at the screen, thinking about what to say, another message pops up.

What about ice cream? Are we out?

This brings a smile to my face. Dad promised me that we'd have an ice cream eating contest this Friday to celebrate me finishing the school year and I'd honestly thought that he'd forgotten with the stress of his job.

We have plenty. I'll get the spoons and stuff ready.

Hopping up, I hurry to the kitchen and start pulling out everything that we need. Three kinds of ice cream, two bowls, two spoons, and all of the toppings you could want. I tap my finger on my chin and dig out the box of sprinkles, setting it down on the counter. I know that a lot of my friends think that it's kinda weird how close I am with my dad, but they don't get it.

When you lose one parent and the other one is the only thing helping you get through it, you grow closer to them. My dad and I don't always see eye-to-eye but he's there for me.

I scoop three flavors of ice cream into each bowl and top them with chocolate sauce, sprinkles, cherries, and even some nuts I found in the back of the cupboard. By the time my dad walks in from the garage, I'm done and I hold out a bowl for him, sticking a spoon into the top of it so that it sticks straight up like a flag.

"I hope that you're ready," I tell him. "Because I'm starving for something other than an ice-cold burrito. I warn you, I'm going to clean out my bowl first."

My dad takes it and then eyeballs it before looking at

me. "Did you leave any ice cream for later?" When I grin at him and nod, he smiles back, kicking off his shoes and following me to the living room. "All right, Lilah, but I have to tell you. Nothing makes me hungrier than digging around in some poor guy's chest cavity."

"Ewww, Dad, gross." I drop down onto the sofa and he flicks on the light before sitting next to me. The remote is between us on the cushions and before I can even move, he grabs it and changes the channel.

"No serial killers before bed," he says firmly, pushing buttons until he comes to a local news channel. "I want to fill my brain with knowledge of the world."

"Serial killers are *from* this world," I tell him, taking a bite of my ice cream. Technically, I'm cheating, since we haven't agreed to start just yet, but if he's going to just sit and talk instead of eat then that's not my fault. "Maybe I want to be a psychiatrist and I'm just learning the signs to look out for."

"Don't do that." He eyeballs me and picks up his spoon. "Ready?"

"Don't do what?"

"Be a psychiatrist. The world is crazy enough without you actively searching for it to come to you. There's no reason to put yourself in that situation." He smiles but I know what he's trying to say.

Maybe if mom hadn't worked such long hours then she'd have noticed the signs of her cancer earlier. If she hadn't been so wrapped up in figuring out other people's problems then she might have realized sooner that she had troubles of her own. Maybe we'd still have her.

But the maybe game is a dangerous one, and one that I decided a long time ago that I'm done playing. It's too easy to get sucked into it and start to wonder how you could

9

have changed your entire life with a single different decision.

"All right," I tell him, not wanting to get into a fight. "We'll talk about that later, after I kick your butt."

"Sure. Go." He shoves a huge bite of ice cream into his mouth and I laugh, then follow suit. My head hurts instantly from the cold, but I power through, gobbling down the moose tracks, very cherry, and mint chocolate chip that fills my bowl. As I eat, I drag my eyes from my dad to look at the TV.

The local news isn't very exciting, but it's better than watching my dad slowly beat me at this contest.

A young reporter stands at the edge of the woods, her face drawn and tired, and I can tell just from looking at her that she'd rather be anywhere else right now. Reaching down to the sofa, I grab the remote and point it at the TV, turning up the sound so that we can hear it better.

"At first, police assumed that the man had simply had an accident and gone over the waterfall, but now questions are being raised about how he really died." Her voice cuts through the silence in our living room and when my dad reaches for the remote, I hold it out of his reach.

"Lilah, this is not what we need to watch right now," he says, but I flap my hand at him.

"You wanted local news," I say. "It doesn't get much more local than this."

I'm right and he knows it. Our house butts right up to the woods that she's standing in front of. I want to rush to the window and look out to see if I can see her, but I have a feeling that if she were that close I'd have noticed the news trucks. The woods stretch on forever and she could be anywhere along where the trees encroach on the town.

"Dressed in a full suit, the man obviously wasn't

prepared for waterfall climbing. This leads authorities to believe that there may have been foul play involved. They are also not ruling out suicide at this time. Anyone with any information about the case is strongly encouraged to come forward." She pauses and touches her ear piece, tilting her head to the side a little bit as she listens.

When she looks back up at the camera, her expression has changed. "I've been told that the authorities have just given us permission to release the victim's name."

The live shot cuts away and the picture of a man fills our TV. He's younger, with a bit of gray around his temple, and grinning at the camera as if whoever took the picture just told a great joke. I don't know him but I feel my stomach twist a little bit. In his photo he looks so happy and full of life. It's hard to believe that he's now dead.

"Victor Ross."

My dad says the man's name before the TV reporter. His bowl of ice cream is totally forgotten in his lap, and he leans forward, his eyes glued to the screen.

"Victor Ross was found in the river below the Widow-maker Falls," the reporter continues. "Drowning in the falls is quite common, but the fact that he was not dressed for a hike has aroused the suspicion of the authoritiesof the possibility of foul play, however they are not ruling out the possibility of suicide. The location of the deceased as well as the circumstances lead them to believe that Mr. Ross may, sadly, have taken his life. Again, anyone with any information about his death should come forward and contact Detective Blake."

A phone number flashes on the screen and I turn to look at my dad.

"You knew him?" I ask, doing my best to sound calm. It's one thing for there to be a dead man on the news, but it's another thing entirely for my dad to know him. I don't know why, but it just seems weird.

"I operated on him a few years ago," he says, giving his head a little shake. "Needed a heart transplant and I did it. Don't you remember? It was a huge deal in the press that the surgery was performed here at our little hospital."

I do remember, now that he mentions it. I remember my dad agonizing over the surgery and even being interviewed on the news about it.

"Was he..." I twirl my finger by the side of my head to get my point across and my dad shakes his head.

"No, not at all. Had just gotten married, wanted kids, the whole nine yards." My dad looks pale as he stares at the screen. The man's picture is still there, but the reporter is still talking over it.

"So why would he kill himself?" I ask the question that I'm sure everyone in town is asking right now. If he was really as stable and happy as my dad is saying, then why in the world would he want to end it all?

The reporter's voice cuts through my thoughts. "Mrs. Ross maintains that her husband would not have killed himself. Police found a bottle of water at the scene of his death and are, at her urging, testing it."

My dad turns to me and swallows hard before answering. "That's just it, Lilah. He wouldn't."

GREY

*A*ll night last night I couldn't get Victor's face out of my mind. He'd been so sick when I met him, but then we did the transplant and he bounced back better than any of us could have expected. I gave him back his life and he promised me that he was going to do everything he could to make his second chance count.

And, from what I now gather in the paper, he did just that.

He was head of the local board for improving living conditions on the poorer side of town. He ran for city council and was elected, and spent his weekends coaching little league. Apparently he played ball in college but hurt his shoulder enough times that he never was going to make it to the big leagues.

He also had a kid, a little boy, who was named after him.

It's too sad to continue reading and I shut the paper right as Lilah walks into the kitchen. She's already on her phone, her fingers flying as she taps out a message to someone, although I have no idea who in the world she could be talking to at seven in the morning.

With a heavy sigh, she sits down at the counter next to me and I push the paper towards her. "Want to do the crossword?"

She shakes her head. "What do you say to waffles downtown?" She puts her phone down on the counter as she asks. Her fingers are still resting on the back of it like she's not entirely ready to let it go, and she tilts her head at me a little as she waits for my response.

"Waffles, but no phones. Deal?" Ever since Lilah got a phone, she's been getting more and more addicted to it. I get that kids her age want to be able to stay connected to each other, but if I have to hear one more TikTok video playing from her room when I head to bed, I think that I'm going to go crazy.

"Deal." She taps her phone with finality, like she's telling it that she'll be back later, then gives me a grin. "You're buying."

"I didn't know that there was an alternative," I laugh, pushing back from the counter and grabbing my keys. Main Street will probably be a nightmare right now, but if my girl wants waffles and is willing to leave her phone behind to get them, then I'm not going to pass up on the opportunity to spend time with her.

We drive in silence, her switching radio stations to find something that isn't playing oldies, and me staring out the window, trying to remember the last time that I saw Victor.

I know that I shouldn't be so torn up about him dying, but I can't help it. The idea makes me ill. I know how hard it is to lose a spouse, how you seem to lose yourself at the same time. No matter how many people visit you and try to make you feel better, there's a huge part of you that dies, too, and you're lost.

Part of me wants to reach out to his widow, but I know that it wouldn't do anything to help. She has to somehow work through what's going on by herself. The last thing that she needs is a stranger trying to contact her when they didn't even really know her husband.

We pull up in front of Mike's Diner and Lilah hops out, stretching her arms over her head before heading for the door. "I'll get us a table," she calls over her shoulder, then disappears inside.

I sit for a moment in the car before circling around to find a parking space. The last thing that I want right now is waffles in a busy diner, but this will be a good distraction. Victor's death shouldn't be affecting me like this, but it's obvious that it's bringing up memories of Sara that I haven't totally dealt with.

"Grey Bennett?" Right as I'm approaching the front door of the diner, someone calls my name.

I turn, craning my neck to see who's behind me. A woman with lovely blue eyes stares at me like she can't believe her good luck of running into me.

"I'm sorry," I say, reaching out automatically to take her hand. "I don't know that we've met."

"Oh goodness, I'm so rude." She takes my hand and squeezes it hard before giving it a little shake and then letting it go. "I'm Carol Matthews, Lilah's math teacher. I think that I've seen you at open house once or twice before, but I wasn't entirely sure if it was you."

"Oh, of course," I say mechanically, even though I don't recognize the woman at all. There's something familiar about her face, but I wouldn't have been able to tell you that the woman was Lilah's teacher on a bet. "Lovely to meet you. Lilah spoke highly of your class even though math wasn't ever her strongest subject."

The woman presses her lips together. "Oh. Lilah didn't tell you?" she asks, and I feel my stomach drop.

"Didn't tell me what?" My daughter and I are close, but I know that there's going to be more and more things that she doesn't want to tell me as she gets older. I can respect that, but if she's keeping a secret about school then that's a problem.

"She needs summer help on her math if she's going to be allowed to move on to Algebra 2 next year," the teacher says. "But it's fine. I told her that I'd be thrilled to help her out and meet with her a couple of times a week to make sure that she was prepared for her exam at the end of the summer."

"I had no idea that she was having problems," I say, giving my head a little shake. "Are you sure that we're talking about the same person?" I don't want this woman to think that I don't believe her, but I have no reason to think that Lilah would keep something like this from me.

Especially because she had to know that I'd find out eventually.

"I'm sure—" she starts to say, but just then Lilah runs up behind me, clapping her hand down on my shoulder.

"Our table's ready, Dad! We kinda cut to the front of the line a little bit because I know the hostess. You coming?" Her voice falters when she notices who I'm talking to. "Oh, Mrs. Matthews...hi."

The teacher gives my daughter a small smile but then turns right back to me. "As I was saying, Dr. Bennett, I'm happy to tutor Lilah throughout the summer so that she doesn't risk getting held back in the fall. She really needs to move on to Algebra 2 with the rest of her class."

"Lilah?" I ask, turning to my daughter. My sweet girl looks pale, her eyes locked on her teacher like she's never seen her before. "When were you going to tell me that you needed help in math?"

"I thought that I could handle it on my own," Lilah mumbles, her eyes darting between me and her teacher. "I appreciate the offer, Mrs. Matthews, but there's no reason for you to have to give up your summer for me. I'm sure that you have better things to do."

"Nonsense." Any animosity that I thought I sensed in the teacher disappears and she grins at my daughter like she honestly can't think of anything better to do with her summer than tutor her. "I love helping my students reach their full potential."

"We'll pay you, of course," I say, and she inclines her head graciously a little towards me.

"Thank you. As I'm sure you're aware, teacher salaries are..." she pauses, trying to come up with the best word. "Somewhat lacking. How does Monday morning sound? Eight o'clock?"

I can feel Lilah trying to burn a hole in the side of my head with her eyes, but I ignore her and shake her teacher's hand again. "Sounds perfect. Thank you again for doing this. I had no idea that Lilah was having trouble, but knowing that you're going to be there to help her out is a huge relief. Thank you again."

"It's my pleasure. Enjoy your waffles." She gives us each a smile and then turns, disappearing quickly into the crowd.

"I literally can't believe that this is happening," Lilah moans, grabbing my arm and pulling me with her to the restaurant. "Summer tutoring? Such a nightmare."

"And *I* 'literally can't believe' that you didn't tell me that you were having so much trouble in math," I counter, pulling back and turning around for a moment. My eyes search the crowd for her teacher, but she's already gone.

Even though she said that she knew me from open house, I can't shake the feeling that I actually know her from somewhere else. There's just something about her that seems incredibly familiar, but I can't put my finger on it.

Matthews. I'm certain that I've never met anyone with that last name before, so it's not like I know her husband. I'll have to think about it. I'll probably sit bolt upright in bed in the middle of the night and remember exactly where I've met her before.

But first, waffles. As much as I want to know where I know my daughter's math teacher from, there are more pressing matters at hand. I turn back to Lilah.

"Fresh fruit or extra syrup?"

LILAH

$\mathcal{M}$y dad left for work at six this morning, but not before he'd come into my room and pulled the covers off of me, crowing like a rooster.

"Happy summer vacation!" he'd cried, dropping my math book and a fresh notebook on my bed. "Looks like it's going to be a relaxing summer full of learning."

"This is terrible," I groaned, rolling over and covering my head with my pillow. "I so can't believe this is happening!"

He'd laughed at me and told me to be polite before disappearing from my room. Even as he went downstairs, I could hear him whistling.

Now I'm at the kitchen table just waiting for the microwave clock to click over to eight in the morning. I have no doubt that Mrs. Matthews will be here right on time, eager to get started and torture me.

This is not how I imagined spending my summer break. I wanted to be hanging out with friends, going to the pool, even just lying in the hammock listening to music. But no.

Instead I'll be here, at the kitchen table, two mornings a week, working with Mrs. Matthews on my algebra.

Not that there's anything wrong with her, really. She's actually always been really nice to me and I always got along with her, even though some people had said that she was mean. It's just that the thought of having to do algebra all summer long is enough to make me sick.

I'm nursing my coffee with extra sugar and cream when there's a brisk knock on the door. Taking a last gulp, I drop my mug in the sink on my way to the front door, wiping my hands on my jeans. I'm nervous for some reason, like I've never had to deal with her before.

It's weird, seeing her at school every day felt normal, but now that she's going to be in my house, everything feels off. Pushing that strange feeling from my mind, I plaster a huge smile on my face and swing open the door.

Mrs. Matthews is dressed like she always is, in khaki pants and a button-up shirt, with a cardigan sweater draped over her shoulders. Her small diamond earrings sparkle in the early morning sun that's creeping up over the roof of our neighbor's house across the street. In one hand she's clutching a travel mug and in the other she has a tote bag stuffed full of books.

I can smell her coffee from here. At least she isn't going to care if I have some myself while we work.

"Good morning," I say, remembering my manners. "Thanks so much for coming here to help me."

"Not a problem," she says, pushing past me into the house. Her heavy tote bag bumps my knees and I wince but she doesn't even notice so I don't say anything. "Happy to help out a student with a promising future. The last thing that we want is for you to get off track and not reach your full potential."

Pausing inside the entryway, she looks around, turning slightly as she takes it all in.

It's the first time in a long time that someone new has been in our house and I try to see it through her eyes. The sofa is old and probably needs to be replaced, but it was one that my mom had picked out years ago and neither my dad or I want to give it up. Everything else, though, is updated and pretty new.

A huge chandelier hangs from the center of the ceiling, shining light on the sofa as well as on the bookcases that line the room. There's a huge globe on a pedestal in the far corner of the room, but her eyes barely flick over it before landing on the photographs above the sofa.

I watch as she sucks in a breath, then walks across the living room, still holding onto both her coffee and her tote bag. Her eyes skim over the pictures before her gaze locks on to the large one in the center.

It was taken right before my mom's cancer diagnosis. She looks tired in it, but also really happy. Her arms are around me and my dad is leaning over her shoulder, the three of us grinning at the camera. The photo was taken at the beach and the ocean is visible behind us.

"This is your mom?" she asks quietly, peering forward to look at it. For a moment, I can't find my voice to answer. I stare at the photo and really look at my mom. It's been hanging there for so long that I've just gotten used it being there and stopped actually seeing it. When was the last time that I really took a good look at it?

"That's her," I say, walking up next to her. She glances at me and then looks back at the picture.

"You poor kid, to lose her when you were so young." Her voice is kind but I bristle at her words. One of the things that I hate more than anything in the world is when people pity me for losing her. Yes, it was terrible, and sure, I'd do anything in the world to bring her back. But missing her isn't going to make her come back to life. And being reminded of how terrible it was to lose her doesn't really help, either.

"It was awful," I say, then lightly touch my teacher on the elbow. "If you want to come with me into the kitchen, I thought that we could work in there." Even as I say it, though, I glance down at my watch.

She's supposed to be here for two hours. Two hours of algebra one-on-one with my teacher. I can't think of anything worse right now. Is there really any harm in standing and talking about my mom for a minute? Any time that we spend talking instead of working means that I'm going to have fewer problems that I'm going to have to work through.

"Sure, sure," Mrs. Matthews says, taking a step towards the kitchen. She's still looking at our family picture, however, and I have a flash of inspiration.

"Do you want to see more pictures of her?" I have no idea where the question came from, and there's no reason that she'd want to see pictures of my dead mom, so I'm surprised when she turns to me with a smile on her face.

"I'd love to," she says. Her smile doesn't quite reach her eyes, so I'm not entirely sure what she's thinking right now, but I realize that I don't care.

Honestly, the last thing that I want to do right now is math, and if I can pull out some family albums and burn a little more time before we really get down to it, then that's exactly what I'm going to do. The thought that my dad won't be happy with me briefly runs through my mind but I push it away.

There isn't any chance that he's going to find out, and

he said to be polite, right? He's at work, saving lives, and if I can distract my teacher just enough to make this morning not as horrible as I thought it was going to be, then I'm going to do it.

"Have a seat," I say, gesturing at the sofa. "I'll be right back with some photos I think you'll love to see."

I walk out of the living room to go to my dad's room. He keeps most of the photo albums tucked away in there so that random visitors don't just grab them and flip through them. I didn't understand at first, but I think that I get it now. The last thing that he wants is for just anyone to pick up the albums and look at mom.

"Sounds wonderful," Mrs. Matthews calls after me. "I'll just wait right here."

Her voice is so happy and light that I almost feel bad for thinking it was weird that she was coming to our house. She's not so terrible, really. In fact, it might be kinda nice to have her around twice a week, as long as we don't get stuck actually doing algebra the whole time.

CAROL

I'm on my third cup of coffee—at Lilah's insistence—and we've made our way through most of the photo albums that she's carted back down the hall from their hiding spot in her father's room. I would have liked to have been able to look through them without her here, but she's right next to me, leaning over my arm to point at pictures while she talks.

I get that she's excited. Getting to talk about your dead mother to someone who is actually listening and not screaming at you to shut up has to be thrilling.

But I wish that she'd let me look on my own.

On the surface, they look like the perfect all-American family. Nobody would ever have guessed that her mother was sick, that something terrible was growing in her undetected. That's the problem with cancer. There's a reason they say it's a...well, you know. Rhymes with witch.

How in the world is the average person supposed to guess that someone they love is ill? That's why you take them to professionals. You put your trust in them, hoping they'll be able to help you and your loved one through whatever is coming.

Sometimes they can.

And sometimes you make a mistake and choose the wrong doctor.

I feel the darkness showing on my face and I have to remind myself to relax. There's no need for Lilah to see anger etched between my eyebrows. This time right now is all about her and I have to remind myself that I don't really matter.

All that matters is getting to know her and her father better, and making sure that she can actually move on to Algebra 2.

Or, at least, that's what I'm telling people.

Lilah points to a wedding picture of her parents, chattering away excitedly about the day. She wasn't even there, not yet a twinkle in her father's eye, but she's heard the stories so many times she knows all of the details.

I know what it's like to walk down the aisle. I know how exciting it is to see the man who you love standing there, his eyes locked on you and only you.

I know what it's like to promise to love him in sickness and in health.

I was only twenty-one when I got married. Everyone told me that I was too young and that we wouldn't ever make it, but George and I loved each other more than anything We got married in my parent's backyard. My little sister stood at my side, and he had his best friend from school standing with him. We said our vows, promising to always be there for each other.

And we were. We grew up and George got a good job working at a local factory. It was long hours and he was tired when he came home, but I was always there to make sure that he was taken care of. Everything was great, we were happy, we were healthy, and then he turned thirty.

Like someone had flicked a switch, he started to feel tired during the day. Often he would come home from work and have to rest before going back and finishing his shift. We went from doctor to doctor, trying to figure out what was wrong.

The first one told us that it was just stress and George was working too hard, so he changed positions within the factory, and cut back on how much he was working. The stress didn't really decrease, but our income did.

So I became a teacher.

My new job helped with the family finances, but it didn't really help George. He was treated for anemia, sleep problems, and depression. Nothing worked and I had to watch helplessly as my husband got more and more tired. He had gotten to the point that he was struggling to make it through the day when one of his friends made an off-hand remark that something might be wrong with his heart.

His friend was right.

George was placed on the transplant list immediately, and there wasn't anything that we could do but wait and pray. When we got a heart we cried for the person who donated it, but inside I was secretly elated. I had to have my George with me, and if that meant that someone else had to die, then I was fine with it.

Nobody else loved their spouse the way that I loved George. These pictures of Lilah's parents are nice, but they didn't have the kind of love that George and I did. I just know it.

The day of the transplant, I couldn't have been more excited. The thought of having my George back the way he used to be, of not having to worry about him being tired all the time, was incredible. I wanted to take him to a larger hospital for the surgery, but George insisted that he stay here. He wanted to be close to our friends and didn't want me to have to uproot my life and stay in a hotel while he recovered.

George wasn't worried. The cardiologist we went to—one Dr. Grey Bennett—was supposed to be the best in the area. The doctor looked me in the eyes and promised me that he would take care of my husband.

And what happened?

He let George die.

Icy fingers grip the back of my neck when I remember the doctor coming out to tell me that George didn't make it. "I'm so sorry," he'd said, "but he was too weak for the surgery. I did everything that I could, but there simply wasn't any way for him to pull through."

One apology, that's all, and my George was cold and dead in the ground.

Dr. Bennett ruined my life on that day. I might still be alive, but the huge part of me that loved George and felt whole because of him is dead and gone. I buried it with him, sure I would never be really happy again.

How I managed to move on from that day, I'll never really know. Yet another doctor told me that I was depressed and prescribed me pills to help me get through everything that I was feeling. It wasn't until I woke up one day and realized that I'd lost half a year of my life that I flushed the pills down the toilet.

After that, instead of sitting around waiting for my life to get better, I swore to myself that I would make it better myself. I'd keep teaching to make sure that I could put food on the table. I downsized to a smaller house so that it was cheaper.

And then I met Trent. Ten years after George died, someone else proposed to me and promised to love me forever. I accepted his proposal, but not because I loved him. Trent is a good man. He takes care of me and wants me to be happy.

What he doesn't know is that there's one thing that I've been promising myself that I'll do since the day that George died: get my revenge on the man who killed him.

The man who's currently staring up at me from the album on my lap.

"So, that's it," Lilah says with a little shrug, grabbing the album and snapping it back. She looks nervous and then smiles at me. "As much as I'd like to not do algebra at all, I have a pretty good feeling that my dad will be really upset if we don't do something other than look at photos and drink coffee while you're here."

"It'll be our little secret," I tell her, leaning forward and grinning like the two of us are partners in crime. "You don't tell your dad that we spent an hour looking at photos and I won't either. But you're right." I plant my hands on my thighs and push up from the sofa. My joints ache when I do this and I rub my knees.

It's a reminder that I'm not as young as I used to be, and I know that time is ticking if I'm going to take care of the Dr. Bennett problem. As much as I'd like to really stretch this out with him, I don't think that I have a full year, like I'd hoped.

"I brought plenty for us to do," I say, and her face falls. She's a sweet girl, it's too bad that she has a monster for a father. "Don't worry, Lilah, I have a few tricks up my sleeve that will have you knocking out problems left and right in no time."

"Excellent!" She hops off the sofa and leads the way

into the kitchen, talking excitedly. I wait until she's turned the corner, then flip an album open and pull out a wedding picture.

They look so happy together. Just like me and my George. My lips curl in disgust as I look at them and I tuck the photo carefully into my tote bag before following Lilah's voice into the kitchen.

GREY

*B*y the time I get home from work, I'm so exhausted that I wish I'd stopped at a drive-thru and gotten takeout for the two of us for dinner. The absolute last thing that I want to do is cook right now, but news of the cardiologist eating at Big Bob's Burgers would spread like wildfire. Lord knows, the sugary coffees are bad enough.

I have to admit, that's one thing that I love about work conferences out of town. Nobody knows who you are when you're in a bigger city, and they sure don't judge you for getting something greasy in a sack when you want a burger and fries.

Something I learned about cardiologists as a whole a long time ago is that we all love greasy food. But we can't very well tell our patients not to eat it and then go ahead and scarf down a double burger with special sauce ourselves, now can we?

"Lilah?" I call, stepping into the house. Her loud rock music thrums from upstairs and I give my head a sad little shake. Whatever band she's in love with this week is a far cry from the classical that we play in the operating room. "I'm home!"

She doesn't answer and I set my keys and wallet on the hall table before wandering into the kitchen. To my surprise, a wave of delicious smells hits me square in the face as I walk through the door. I pause, trying to figure out what happened.

Whose kitchen am I in right now?

There's something in the oven, I can tell from the way that the timer is blinking down, and she's actually set the table with real plates and silverware. I let myself run my fingers over the fork nearest to me before walking to the oven and pulling it open to look in.

A huge roast surrounded by potatoes, carrots, and onions greets me and I raise my eyebrows, shutting the door and turning around to look for the hidden camera. There's no way that my daughter did all of this on her own. She's claimed allergies to cooking before and I'm sure that she survives on pb&j sandwiches while I'm at work.

"Lilah?" Running my hand along the banister, I head upstairs. The music is louder now and I can't help but roll my eyes a little when I knock on her door. How she can hear me over the sound of someone screaming about how much he really does love the girl he cheated on, I don't know, but a moment later the music clicks off and she opens the door.

At first, I'm pretty convinced that this girl isn't my daughter.

She looks like her, sure. She has the same hair and face, and the way that she's standing with one hip jutted out and her hand resting on it is just like her mother used to do when she was making a point. But this doppelgänger is wearing an apron, which is something that she listed towards the top of her allergy list that day when I'd asked her to help me cook.

"You're wearing an apron and there's a roast in the oven," I say, unable to stop myself from stating the obvious. "You want to talk about that?"

I fully expect her to scowl and tell me that I'm being ridiculous, but to my surprise she grins and then gives me a twirl, putting on a little fashion show. "What do you think? I found it in a drawer. I think that I remember mom wearing this one."

Reaching out, I finger the frilled fabric that runs around the neck. "Yep," I say, doing my best to keep my face neutral. Lilah hates it when I get emotional about her mom. I don't think she realizes just how much I miss her. "Your mom loved this one. That, and the one tucked even farther in the back of the drawer."

Lilah frowns. "What does that one look like? I don't remember."

"Never mind. It has a dirty word on it." I wink at my daughter, who grins, then darts around me, running for the stairs. "Don't run down the stairs," I call, but she's already taking them two at a time, wanting to beat me to the kitchen so she can see exactly what the apron says.

I follow her, turning into the kitchen right as she pulls the apron in question from the back of the drawer. She holds it up in front of her and then breaks into a grin. "I can't believe that you guys owned this," she says, turning it so that I can see it. "You told me that I can't use that word."

I shrug. "You can't. But if you're going to cook, then you can wear the apron." Her face lights up and I hold up a finger to stop her from interrupting. "But only when we don't have guests. I can't let anyone know that my daughter knows that word."

She rolls her eyes. "I rode the bus in middle school, Dad. Don't try to pretend that I don't know this word, and even worse." She folds up the apron and stashes it back in the drawer, turning to me and crossing her arms. "Isn't there something that you want to say?"

"You mean like how it smells so amazing in here?" Grabbing a fork, I open the oven door and poke at the roast, pulling back a bit to shred the meat. It shreds perfectly and my mouth waters at the smell. This is going to be amazing, and I'm going to do whatever it takes to make sure that Lilah cooks like this for me on a regular basis. "So what's the story? Did you get sick? Are you feverish? Can I get you something for your allergies?"

"You're hysterical." She grabs a pitcher of water with lemon slices from the fridge and fills up the two glasses on the table while she talks. "No, after I finished my algebra this morning, Mrs. Matthews helped me throw it together. She said that she's always enjoyed cooking and was happy to show me how to do it." She shrugs, her shoulders a little too thin under her shirt. "It was kinda fun. I guess."

"Kinda fun," I repeat, carrying the roast over to the table. We have rolls in the bread box and I grab two, tossing them in the microwave to heat up. "Well, I can't tell you how thrilled I am to come home to something that smells and looks so amazing. Thank you. And your mom would be very proud, you know."

Lilah ducks her head away from me but not before I see the smile on her face. "Well, don't get used to it or anything. If you make it weird, I'll stop."

"Fair enough." We sit and say grace, then I let her serve herself before speaking again. "So, tell me. How was math? I mean, I love that you two made us something to eat, but I hope that you knocked out some problems, too."

"Oh my God, so many problems." She blows on a carrot, pops it into her mouth and swallows before continuing. "Don't worry, Dad, Mrs. Matthews said that I'm sure to be fine to go to Algebra 2 this fall as long as I keep it up. She left some homework and I completed it already."

This makes me stop and stare at my daughter. It's not that I don't think that she's capable enough, she's just never showed much interest in really applying herself and going above and beyond. Guilt stabs at the back of my mind that it took someone I don't even know to get Lilah interested in cooking, but I don't let myself dwell on that.

It wasn't for lack of trying, that's for sure. She never said as much, but I always knew that she wished her mom could have been the one to teach her to cook, not me.

Part of me idly wondered from time to time if I should date, if I should try to make our family whole again. Now it's been so long that I can't imagine ever sitting across from anyone other than my daughter at dinner. I can't imagine trying to change our family to make room for someone else.

No, even though I'm tired of being alone, Lilah and I have a good thing going here, just the two of us. If she has lucked into a good role model in Mrs. Matthews, maybe it will all work out okay.

"So, tell me about her. Mrs. Matthews, I mean." I swear that I recognized her outside the hospital, but I still can't put my finger on where I've met her before. There's something about her face that's familiar, but try as I might, I can't think of where I actually know her from.

Maybe she just has one of those faces.

"She's great," Lilah says. "She was super friendly and asked questions to get to know me better before we got started. I mean," she continues, stabbing a piece of meat and blowing on it, "I was in her class, so she does know me, but this felt like she really cared, you know?"

Nodding, I listen as my daughter rambles on about her day. It sounds like it was a really good one, that she got the help and attention that she's been needing and craving. I wish that I could be here for her more than I am, but sometimes you have to make sacrifices. Everything that I've ever done has been for my daughter, but I realize with a start that there's one more thing that I can do to that will help her out.

CAROL

*E*arly Tuesday morning, Trent has already disappeared into the back yard to work on his putting and I'm cleaning up the kitchen. It's just like any other morning.

I rinse the plates, watching as the water mixes with the maple syrup and rinses it away before it finally runs down the drain. Next, I load the dishwasher, making sure that none of the plates touch. I wouldn't want them to get chipped by accident during the cycle.

Once that's running I wipe down the counters and start making my grocery list for the afternoon. It's the same every day. By making sure that I follow my routine and don't deviate from it, I can ensure that I don't have too much time to stop and think about the past.

Trent's great. Honestly. He's fine. He's taken care of me and I know that he loves me.

But he's not George. There won't ever be another George and the fact that he was taken away from me makes it difficult for me to breathe some days, even all these years later.

A loud snap pulls me from my thoughts and I look down at the counter in surprise. The pencil that was in my hand is now in two pieces and I get up, taking them straight to the trash. If they're not perfect, I don't want them. I need everything in my life to be as perfect as possible.

In the drawer by the sink, I have twenty more pencils, all freshly sharpened. I pick the first one out and test the tip on my finger. Yes. Sharp enough to write.

My grocery list finished, I'm about to get up and start the laundry when my cell phone rings. It's plugged in over by the pencil drawer and I freeze for a moment, staring at it, wondering who might be calling on a Tuesday morning.

For the longest time after George died, I imagined that he would come back to me one day. Each time the phone rang I hoped that it would be him on the other end of the line, telling me how much he loved me. It won't ever happen, but I can't help it. It's what I want.

Unknown number, reads the screen. My stomach twists hard and I feel my throat threatening to close up as I tap the green answer button.

"Hello?" My voice comes out froggy and weak, so I clear my throat and try again. "Hello? Who is this?"

There. Better. *Stronger.* Not the voice of someone you can take advantage of.

"Is this Mrs. Matthews? It's Grey Bennett." His voice snakes out of the phone and wraps around me like a heavy, wet blanket. I shiver violently, wanting to break free from it. You can tell a lot about people from their voice. You can tell if they're kind or not, how happy they are in life, if they're the type of person to help out a stranger or just pass on by.

I can tell that Grey Bennett is a murderer.

Part of me wonders if I'd know that if I didn't already know the truth about him, but I can't think about that right now, so I push that thought from my mind and plaster a huge smile on my face.

"Always smile when you're talking to people," my psychologist had told me once. "It'll come through in your tone and they'll think that you're really happy to hear from them."

"Dr. Bennett! What a pleasant surprise. How are you this morning?" Turning, I lean back against a corner of the counter. It digs through my shirt into my lower back and I suck in my breath at the pain, but I don't move. It's grounding, more than anything.

"I'm wonderful, just heading in to work. I wanted to call and thank you for what you did with Lilah yesterday." His voice cuts in and out and if I close my eyes I can picture him in his car.

"The math? Not a problem at all." I force out a little laugh and then look down at the check on the counter. Lilah had pressed it into my palm yesterday before I left, telling me that her dad would be really upset if she forgot to pay me. "Thank you for the check."

"Well," he says, with a chuckle, "I didn't know that your services included somehow getting my daughter to cook. Dinner was amazing, but I don't want you to feel like that's something that you have to do every single day. You're her math tutor, and while I appreciate it, I don't want to impose."

I force a laugh. "You didn't, Dr. Bennett. Lilah is delightful and I love to cook." Turning, I see Trent through the window. "Believe me, the kitchen is one of my favorite places to be. Can't think of anywhere else I'd have rather been yesterday."

"Well, you're a lifesaver. Yesterday was a long one for

me and that roast was amazing to come home to. And, please, call me Grey. You're not my patient."

His words send a prickle of anxiety up my back. No, I'm not his patient, and I won't ever be. In fact, I pity anyone who looks up from the operating table and sees that man standing over them.

"Okay, then Grey," I manage. "But is it all right with you if I help Lilah in the kitchen from time to time when we've finished her math? She said yesterday that she wished she had someone to teach her how to cook."

He pauses and I wonder if he's focused on the road or if he knows that I'm lying. Lilah hadn't said anything of the sort yesterday, but I can tell she's starved for a woman to pay attention to her. From what she's said, Grey is an amazing father, but that doesn't take the place of a mother. Every child needs both a mother and a father.

Grey lost his daughter's mother, and I'm sorry for that for her sake, but he took my children's father from them. He's the one who took George from me. What's that they say about karma?

"Of course," he says, and I breathe a sigh of relief. It's not that I really love helping Lilah learn how to cook, which is something that she should already know at her age, but this way I'm going to be able to continue with my plan. "You're great, Mrs. Matthews, and please let me know if I'm not paying you enough. You're really doing more than what we agreed to."

"Not a problem, not a problem." Through the window I can see Trent walking back to the house, so I need to wrap this up. "I'll be there on Thursday, like we discussed. Mondays and Thursdays."

"Oh, that's another thing," he says, hurriedly, like he can tell that I'm trying to get off the phone and he wants to stop me before I do. "Is there any possible way that you could come three times a week? This is going to sound silly, but Lilah really loved having you there. It meant a lot to her to work with you in the kitchen and she said that you guys had a lot of fun."

A slow smile spreads across my face even though I want to get off the phone so that Trent can see me hard at work in the kitchen. He doesn't love it when I'm on the phone, even if I'm negotiating a job right now. Not that he would know that. "Three times a week instead of two?" I ask, to verify. "Sounds amazing, Grey. Thanks for calling. I hope you have a good day."

"You too," he says, but I'm already tapping the red dot to hang up on him. As quickly as possible, I put the phone back on its charger and turn around to the counter just as Trent walks in.

"Everything okay?" he asks, giving me a smile. "You look frazzled. Happy. Something. I dunno." He tilts his head, like he can't quite put a finger on it.

"I'm wonderful," I tell him, giving him a beaming smile before walking towards the laundry room. "Just always have things to do, you know."

Trent calls something after me but I ignore him. He's a good man, but he wouldn't ever support what I'm doing right now. As much as I'd love to talk to him about what I've got planned for Grey, I know full well that he wouldn't understand. He's supportive of me working at their house over the summer instead of spending all my free time with him, but he wouldn't understand this.

There's only one person who would, and that's George. I have no doubt in my mind that he would not only have understood what I'm going to do for him, but also would have appreciated it. He would have seen all that I'm doing to remember him and to ensure that nobody else has to suffer the way that he and I did.

It may seem cruel right now, but I'm going to teach Dr. Bennett a little lesson. You can't take people's loved ones from them without any repercussions. He lost his wife, but that wasn't anyone's fault. That was bad luck, a poor deal of the cards.

George's death, though, that wasn't bad luck. Grey Bennett took my husband from me and it's now finally time for him to pay.

LILAH

$\mathcal{I}$ can't believe that my dad is okay with Mrs. Matthews coming over to help me learn more about math and cooking three times a week now! I never thought that I'd be this excited to have someone come over and hang out with me while teaching me things, but I have to admit that it's really nice to have her here, and wanting to get to know me better.

It was a little strange at first on Monday, I'll admit. And having the teacher over to your house doesn't exactly make you cool. But it's like she really wants to get to know me. She made me feel important and really listened, like what I had to say mattered.

I didn't tell my dad how much I liked it, but he must have figured it out. Or else he just really liked having a hot homecooked meal waiting for him when he got home from the hospital. I know that he works long hours in the OR.

Used to be, I'd want him to take me out for a slice of pizza once in a while. Now, though, I don't really care if we go out to eat or not. Having Mrs. Matthews here and knowing that she's going to help me get better in the kitchen is exciting.

I want to make her proud. I want her to see that I'm a fast learner and that I'm better at cooking than I am at math. I'm sure that it sounds silly, but it would feel really good to have someone be so proud of me. I mean, I know Dad is. But he doesn't say it too much.

This morning, when she knocks on the door, I have two mugs of coffee already poured ready for us. I know that we have some math to get through before we can cook, but she promised me that she'd show me how to make a frittata for lunch, telling me that the leftovers would be perfect for my dad for dinner.

The sooner we get through the algebra, the sooner the two of us can just hang out together. That thought makes me excited and I try to ignore the little voice in the back of my head reminding that she's only coming over here because my dad is paying her to.

"Hi, Mrs. Matthews!" I cry, swinging the door wide open for her. She's dressed just the same as she would be at school again today, in pleated khakis and a cardigan. Unlike at school, though, she has on a pretty necklace with a heart pendant that hangs right at the base of her neck. "Oh!" I say, my eyes locking on it. "That's really pretty."

"This?" Her hand flutters up and she lightly touches the locket. A small smile appears on the corners of her lips. "It was a gift from my one true love," she says, stroking it before dropping her hand from it. "I'm glad you like it as much as I do."

"Sounds romantic," I say, unsure of how to respond. Mrs. Matthews is so much older than me, and adults never want to talk to kids about stuff like that. Just that she even told me that she had one true love makes me feel mature.

"Yes." She sniffs the air and then turns to me. "Please tell me that you have some coffee for me."

I grin at her, noticing the way she smiles back, then lead her to the kitchen. I don't remember my mom throwing a lot of parties, but she did entertain from time to time and I feel just like her as I lead my guest through the house. "I made us coffee and put it on the table so we could get right to work."

"Smart girl," she says, hanging her tote bag on the back of the chair and taking a seat. "I like to see you thinking ahead. This tells me that you mean business and want to get through the math so we can start cooking, am I right?"

"Busted," I grin, blushing a little even though I try not to. She nailed it. I sit down next to her, pulling out a sheet of paper. I want so badly for her to like me, but I'm unsure of what to say next. Finally, I come up with something. "Business first, then pleasure," I say, taking a sip of my coffee, feeling quite grownup.

She smiles at me and I swear, I feel myself swoon a little bit. I'm much too old to be acting this excited about someone like her paying attention to me, I know that, but I just can't help it.

"Okay," she says, not wasting any time. I notice that she's taken a sip of the coffee I made but hasn't commented on it yet. I hope that she's not disappointed in what I made. "We're going to start at the beginning and move through lessons quickly, pausing when we run into problems. How does that sound?"

Awful. "Sounds great," I tell her, trying to sound cheery. "I want to get through this quickly and pass the test to get me into Algebra 2. There's no reason why I can't, right?"

She pauses, looking at me over her glasses. They must be readers, because she only ever puts them on in class if she is going to be looking at something close up, never far away. They make her kinda look like an owl. "I think that you're incredibly bright, Lilah," she tells me. "Obviously you got that from your parents. If you work hard and do what I ask, I have no doubt that we can get through this quickly. Now, let's get started."

I swear, her words settle around me and actually make me feel like I'm glowing. It feels so damned good to have someone so confident in me, telling me that I'm going to do a great job. And, as soon as we finish math, we can cook together. Maybe she'll tell me more about her one true love.

I had no idea that math teachers could be that romantic, and I have to admit that I'm a little bit excited to find out more about her. She asked so many questions about my mom and dad on Monday that she's probably expecting me to ask some in return. I've tried to think up some good ones to ask that will show her that I'm interesting and not just another student that she has to hang out with.

I mean, the fact that she wants to meet with me three times a week now and help me learn to cook has to mean something, right? Surely if she only thought that I was an annoying student, she wouldn't feel that way about me. Even though Dad is paying her.

I glance over at her while she pulls out the materials that we're going to be working on today. I tap my pencil on the counter a couple times before she looks over to me.

"Everything okay, Lilah?" "It's great," I tell her with a brisk nod. "Just looking forward to getting started and seeing what the two of us can knock out today." Then I throw her a smile and she returns it.

I might not have been super excited about having to give up some of my summer to learn some math that I was supposed to already know, but I guess that it could be worse. Mrs. Matthews is a lot nicer now than she was when we were in school and I honestly think that she wants to get to know me better.

That feels really, really good. I'll learn from her—both math and cooking—and then I'll get to actually spend some time with my friends at the pool. That was the deal with Dad, after he found out I was doing so badly in math. Get my grades in gear first. Then and only then would I be allowed to hang out with my friends.

Honestly, I don't see how this situation could possibly work out any better.

CAROL

*J*finish up the day with Lilah and sit in my car in her driveway for a few minutes while I try to think of what I'm going to do next. I still have a few hours before Trent expects me home to make him some dinner. Honestly, you'd think that by now a grown man like himself would be able to come up with food to eat, but he's useless.

Well, I certainly didn't marry him for love or because I thought that he was going to be good in the kitchen. I only married him because it was not appropriate for a widowed woman without children not to remarry. The last thing that I needed was for anyone to think that I was up to anything. So I married the first man who looked my way.

He's not unkind, really, it's just that nobody could ever possibly hold a candle to my George. When I lost him, I felt like I lost part of my soul. I still ache for him every single day, although I don't tell anyone that.

Nobody would understand how I feel, and to be honest people would probably notice me more if I talked about how I feel. As it is, nobody notices the older math teacher. I dress to fly under the radar, and it works. If people do look at me then their eyes tend to slide right back off of me. Suits me fine. That way, I can continue my really important work.

Lilah had been overeager to please this morning, which meant that the math got finished quickly, but it also meant that she wanted me to work with her in the kitchen. I'm happy to help and think sometimes that I should have been a home ec. teacher. Unfortunately, that was what every other young girl my age wanted to be, so I chose math instead.

It all worked out in the end, though, because I'm analytical. I can figure out what's going to happen and twist it to make sure that it works for my purpose.

Like right now.

Opening the middle console of my car, I pull out a small spiral notebook. The front half of it is filled with my day-to-day schedule for the past few months: doctor's appointments, trips to the hair salon, when I need to go to the grocery store, and even reminders for church potlucks.

The back of the notebook is filled with grocery lists. Trent ate meat when we first met. Disgusting. It hadn't taken long for me to convince him to go vegetarian. Animals are the one pure thing on this earth and eating them is something that only truly evil people would do.

I was more than happy to show Lilah how to make a roast this week because I know how evil her father is. He'd never understand the value of an animal's life. They never hurt people like he has. They don't deserve to suffer.

Not like he does.

But I'll have the two of them eating vegetarian before long.

Shaking my head to clear it, I flip to the center of my notebook. This is where all of my most interesting stuff is.

At first, I was worried that Trent might stumble upon it, but to do that, he'd actually have to take an interest in what I have written down. That's just not the type of man he is. He'd much rather be hitting golf balls in the back yard then reading anything, even if it is just a list.

A list of names, to be precise.

Victor Ross tops it. I've already scratched his name out with a pen, just a simple line straight through it to remind myself that my work is only partly finished. I still run my finger across the letters of his name, whispering it to myself.

He was a nice guy. Most of them on this list are, from what I've seen. That's why I couldn't really put them in order and come up with a way to plan out who had to die first. All I knew was that they had been given the gift of life, and my George hadn't.

Grey Bennett held all their hearts in his hand. He literally watched and felt them beat. He was able to make sure that they all survived. He saved them. My fingers tremble and I put my hands in my lap so that I don't have to look at them shaking.

And why did he save them? So that they could go on and have wonderful lives with their families. It wasn't fair, not to me, not to my George. It wasn't fair that these patients should all survive and my husband should have to die.

Grey Bennett doesn't even care. He has no idea who I am, no idea that I'm the wife of the man that he murdered so many years ago. George and I had a wonderful life planned out together and it only took one man to take everything that we had planned and ruin it all.

I hate him.

The emotion surges through me so violently that my eyes snap up from the paper and focus on the house. Lilah is in there. She's the one precious thing that Grey still has, and it would be so easy for me to go in there and make him pay. He'd see how terrible my life has been since George died if I did that. If I took her away from him.

But that's not the plan, and if there's one thing that I love, it's a plan.

Taking a deep breath, I close my eyes and chant softly to myself. I don't believe in praying, don't believe in the hocus pocus idea that some man in the sky will help you when you can't seem to help yourself, but I do believe in making sure that I don't act rashly, and chanting is the one thing that helps me to refocus.

After a minute, I open my eyes and look back down at the list in my hand, composed again. Victor may be crossed off, but there are still a lot of names on my list that I have to get to before I will be finished. My finger taps the name under Victor's and a small smile forms at the corners of my mouth.

This isn't some half-cooked idea that I came up with last night. No, I've been doing research for years, ever since my George was put into the ground.

It was easy to follow the Grey Bennett success story. They kept it pretty quiet that he killed George, of course they did, but every single major success that he had went right into the paper. The town couldn't seem to get enough of the handsome young doctor. Transplant after transplant made the news and he actually made quite a name for himself in the surrounding areas.

I'm not interested in people who just had ablations or stents put in, unless I run out of transplant patients to make my point. Stents and ablations are child's play, something that any cardiologist worth his salt could easily do. I'm much more interested in the lives he saved oh-so-heroically, the people he really brought back from the brink of death.

He's done it over and over, getting more and more cocky with each transplant, but he didn't do it for George. Either he had an off day—though when someone's life is in your hands you are not allowed to have an off day—or he just didn't care enough that morning in the operating room. No matter what it was, I have to stop him.

I have to show him that he's not good enough to continue practicing medicine.

He wants to pretend to be God and hold their lives in his hands? I'll teach him a lesson about playing God. I'll show him.

He didn't save George, so why should any of his other patients still be alive?

I repeat the name to myself a few times and then put my notebook away, making sure to flip it shut and tuck it under my winter gloves. As I start the car I repeat the name again, keeping my voice quiet as I do.

It's not a prayer. It's a hunting call.

GREY

I was having the wildest dream last night. My wife and I were back in medical school. She was healthy and we were both so happy.

My stomach clenches when I remember that I won't ever see her again. But instead of getting back into bed and dwelling on it, which is what I would usually do, I pull on a hoodie and slide my feet into slippers, since the house is still chilly, and make my way down the stairs, following the incredible smell of toast, bacon and eggs.

That's the only thing that could get me out of bed before eight on a Saturday.

There's music on in the kitchen, but it's not the screaming rock music that Lilah loves so much. Strange, but I'll take it. It's certainly much more relaxing first thing in the morning.

"I honestly thought that a very polite burglar had broken in and was making me breakfast," I tell my daughter as I walk into the kitchen. She's at the stove in her mom's apron and turns around with a grin, holding the spatula out like a weapon.

"Be nice or I'll burn your eggs."

I hold my hands up in mock surrender and walk over to flick on the coffee pot. It grumbles to life and I turn to my daughter while I wait for it to brew. "Care to tell me what this 4-star treatment is about?"

"Just four?" She wrinkles her nose and plates our food, setting it down on the counter. "I just thought that you would enjoy being pampered a little bit."

"I do," I tell her, "I'm just trying to figure out where it's all coming from." I hold up two mugs inquiringly, Lilah nods, and I pour us each some of the brew. She doctors hers up with cream and sugar and I join her at the counter to eat.

"It's Mrs. Matthews," she tells me, with a dip of her chin. "We talk when we're doing math and cooking in the kitchen, and I kinda got the impression that maybe I could help out here a little bit more. Maybe it wouldn't kill me to do a little cooking so that you could rest, you know? She's a pretty big fan of yours, by the way."

I take a bite of bacon before answering, weighing my words carefully. On the one hand, I'm really glad that my daughter is not only learning the algebra that she desperately needs, but also life skills like being able to turn on the stove without burning down the house.

On the other hand, I'm not entirely sure that I like the two of them talking about me when I'm not here.

Then again, if their conversations result in breakfasts like this, then maybe I should just stop complaining.

"Well, it's delicious, so even if she hated me, I'd be thanking her the next time that I see her. And thank you to you, too." Lilah grins at that and then grabs the remote, turning on the TV.

Having a TV in the kitchen had been my wife's idea. She'd wanted to be able to follow along with her favorite cooking shows and did exactly that before she got too sick. After she died, I'd thought about taking it out so that it didn't act as a crutch when Lilah and I should probably be talking instead.

I missed the short window that I had to do it, though. At first, it had been nice to have it in the kitchen because Lilah was so young when her mom died. Having it there made sure that we didn't just eat in silence all the time. By the time we finally figured out how to talk to each other without her mom there, it was too late to take it out.

We watch the news during breakfast, but TV at night has to wait until after dinner. That's the rule and, so far, we've both done a pretty good job sticking to it.

"Let's see what crazy things are going on this weekend," she says, popping a bite of toast in her mouth. She loves it really well done and she crunches it between her teeth while she stares at the screen.

For a moment I look at my daughter. Every single day she looks more and more like Sara and I just want to hug her and remind her how much I love her. But then I actually hear what's being said on the news and I look away from her, my eyes locked on the screen.

"Police are at the scene of what they're labeling as a horrible accident. Michael Teal, sixty-eight, is dead after running his car in the garage with the door closed behind him. He was found early this morning by his wife, who was worried that he hadn't come home last night after going out with a friend for drinks. In a horrible twist of fate, her husband had indeed come home, but had fallen asleep in the garage while the car was still running. The same type of bottle of water found at the scene of Victor Ross's death was recovered in the vehicle."

"Oh, my God," Lilah whispers, putting her toast down

on her plate and wiping her hands on her napkin. "Don't we know him?"

I nod, unable to speak. I operated on Michael just a few years ago. His heart had been bad from years of hard living and I'd replaced it. I remember how ecstatic he and his wife had been when I performed the surgery and how he'd promised me that he'd change his habits to keep from dying young.

It looks like he didn't change them enough.

"Unfortunately, as most people know, carbon monoxide poisoning can occur incredibly quickly in a closed space, like in a car in a garage with the door closed. When the car is left to idle and the carbon monoxide has no place to go, it can build up to incredibly dangerous levels in a very short period of time. This is, luckily, a painless way to die. More than forty people die each year from carbon monoxide poisoning in the United States, making it a silent killer to watch out for. If you think that you—"

I don't even realize that I'm pointing the remote at the TV until the screen goes black and the sound disappears from the room. For a moment, Lilah and I sit in silence, both of us trying to comprehend what we just heard. She turns to me, like she's going to speak, but then sees my face and gives her head a little shake.

"Michael was a really good guy," I say, finally managing to speak. "A good guy. I honestly can't believe that he'd pass out in the car like that and let this happen to him."

"Do you think that he was drunk?" she asks, finally speaking. "Like, why else would you just...fall asleep like that? His wife said that he'd been out with friends, so, I mean...wow."

I shake my head, still stunned. It was one thing for Victor to drown last week. The police still don't have any leads, although the last I heard, they're still treating it like a homicide. But now for Michael to die this week too?

It doesn't make any sense.

Then again, when you deal with an aging population, at some point, they're going to start dying. You can't keep people alive forever, no matter how hard you try. As much as I'd like to think that I can keep everyone healthy and in one piece forever, even if you replace all of their organs, the body will give up eventually.

Both of the men who died were technically on borrowed time. That doesn't make it any easier for their widows, though. Without thinking, I push back from the counter.

"Breakfast was delicious," I tell Lilah, reaching down to lightly rest my hand on the top of her head. "But I think that I need to go for a run."

"I'll come too." She drops her crumpled napkin on the counter and stands up, looking at me expectantly. "You don't have to go by yourself."

My heart starts pounding in my chest. I know what's about to happen, and I also know that getting out of the house as quickly as possible is the most important thing. I'm about to have a panic attack and I need some fresh air. By myself. Without Lilah asking me every few paces if I'm okay.

"I'd prefer it if you stay home," I tell her. "I promise you that after I get back and shower we can play a board game together, okay? Pick it out."

The disappointment on her face is obvious and I feel a twinge of guilt, but I need to get out of here, out of the house, and I need to get out now. I need the open sky above me and the sidewalk rolling out in front of me if I'm going to be able to catch my breath and stave off this panic attack.

I realize I have nothing to do with Victor and Michael dying, but I knew them both. I don't always remember all of my patients, but seeing their faces on the TV had felt like an electric jolt through my body.

Turning from my daughter, I race to the front closet and yank on running shoes. My head pounds, the two men's faces going around and around like a circus carousel in my mind's eye, until I step out the front door and practically throw myself away from the house and into a run.

LILAH

*D*ad and I didn't speak about Michael Teal's death for the rest of the weekend. He came back from his run Saturday morning sweating and breathing hard. After he took a shower he came downstairs and we played Yahtzee.

Neither one of us mentioned the fact that two of his transplant patients had just died within a week of each other.

It's so strange, but I don't know the questions to ask him to get him to open up to me. He was quieter than usual when he left for work this morning, giving me an extra long hug before getting in his car and backing out of the garage.

I wanted to follow him. I wanted to beg him to stay home and watch movies with me all day, like we used to after mom died and I was taking time off school. He's always been there for me and I hate the fact that I can't be there for him in return now that he needs me. There just isn't anything that I can do for him.

These thoughts are still running through my head when Mrs. Matthews knocks on the front door. Glancing in the mirror on my way to answer it, I rake my fingers through my hair, trying to comb out the mess. I look rough, like I didn't get enough sleep, but I'm not entirely sure that Dad even noticed this morning.

"Good morning," I say brightly when I open the door. There isn't any reason to make Mrs. Matthews worry about me or my dad. What he's going through right now is rough, but I have a pretty good feeling that he wouldn't like it if I told everyone about how torn up he is right now.

"Lilah, how are you?" Mrs. Matthews bustles into the house, a grin on her face, but that slides off quickly when she turns and looks at me. "Oh, darling, are you okay? You look like you just lost your best friend!"

Her voice is so kind, her eyes locked on mine, and she feels so safe and comfortable that I feel myself growing weak. I know that my dad wouldn't want me telling just anyone about what's going on, but Mrs. Matthews isn't just anyone, is she? She's giving up her summer not only to help me learn the math I'm supposed to know, but also to help me learn to cook.

If I can trust anyone, it's her. Besides, if my dad didn't trust her then I don't think that he'd let her into the house three days a week while he was gone.

"Did you watch the local news this weekend?" I ask, doing my best to keep a tremble out of my voice. The last thing that I want is for Mrs. Matthews to think that I'm weak. I need her to see that I'm strong, and crying about the news isn't going to help my case.

"Oh, Lilah, did you know that Mr. Teal who died?" She's so kind, putting her arm around my shoulder and guiding me to the sofa. I melt into her a little bit because it feels so good to have someone caring about me right now, even though part of my brain is telling me that we need to get to the math, that she's not here to be my counselor.

"Not really," I sniff, angrily wiping away the tears that are quickly brimming up in my eyes. And that's the truth—I didn't really know him. So why in the world am I so upset? I think that I'm just picking up on what my dad has been feeling this weekend. I know that he does his best to keep his emotions under control and hidden from me, but it's hard not to notice when he's as silent as he has been this weekend.

"He seemed like a lovely man from what I saw on the news," Mrs. Matthews says consolingly. Her hand is rubbing up and down my back and I actually feel myself starting to relax a little bit. It feels good, like she really cares. "Such a shame when accidents like that happen. So pointless."

I nod, sniffing hard, then look at her. She's been nothing but kind since she came here to help me. Even though it feels a little weird, there isn't any reason why I can't trust her.

"He...he was my dad's patient," I finally say, and she looks surprised. Her free hand flutters up to her chest and she waits for me to continue. "My dad performed a heart transplant on him a while back." I force myself to continue. "But that's not all," I hear myself saying. "The man who drowned last weekend, Victor Ross? He was my dad's patient, too."

Mrs. Matthews sucks in a sharp breath. "Your poor father," she says. She sounds so concerned that I just close my eyes and let her words wash over me. It feels really good to have someone here who will actually talk to me about what's going on. "How's he holding up?"

I shrug, unsure of how to answer that honestly. "I'm not

sure," I say. "He tends to be quiet about things that upset him, so he didn't really mention it very much."

"Understandable." She pats my knee. "I imagine that every patient your father loses upsets him terribly, am I right? It has to be so hard for him to know that he did his best but still wasn't able to save someone."

I nod, even though I'm not really sure what my dad would say about that. "He doesn't talk about it, so I don't know," I say, "but how can it not tear him up inside?"

"He never mentions when surgeries go wrong?" Mrs. Matthews leans down and pulls a hankie from her tote bag, pressing it into my hand.

I shake my head. "Not that I can remember. I have no idea how many go wrong, to be honest. Is that pretty common?"

"Hard to say, dear." She loops her arm around me again, pulling me closer to her so that I'm leaning against her side. For a moment, I hesitate, unsure of whether or not she really wants to comfort me, but if she didn't, she wouldn't be holding me like this, right?

It's just so strange to have any adult other than my dad want to hold me like this. It feels good, even though I don't want to admit that to myself. The last woman who comforted me like this when something was terribly wrong was my mom.

"It's so hard for a child to be strong for a parent," she murmurs, and I nod against her shoulder, using her hankie to dab away my tears. "You don't have to be strong, you know that, right? You're still his daughter, not an adult."

"I know." Taking a deep breath, I force myself to sit up. "He doesn't ask me to be strong for him. This weekend was just...well, it was hard. Victor first, then Michael?" I give a little shudder. "I can't imagine what he's going through right now. I'm sure that he feels terrible, even though he had nothing to do with them dying."

"Yes, and the guilt that he'd feel if he was responsible for their death would be even more overwhelming." Mrs. Matthews shakes her head like she can't quite fathom how terrible that would really be. I can't either, and when I try to, all I want to do is cry more.

We sit in silence for another moment, then Mrs. Matthews squeezes my shoulder. "Please tell me that I smell coffee," she says.

I grin at her, wiping my eyes one more time before trying to return the hankie. To my surprise, she takes my hand and closes it around the bit of cloth. "It's yours, Lilah. Keep it, okay? Use it to remember that you don't always have to be strong, darling."

"Thank you," I whisper, even though my throat is tight from crying. I take a good look at the hankie before stuffing it into my pocket. It has gorgeous embroidered flowers around the edges, with cute little yellow bees pollinating them. "I appreciate it."

"If you ever need someone to talk to, Lilah, I can be that person. I don't want you ever to think that I'm trying to take the place of your mom, but I love children and never had any of my own. Maybe you can think of me as an adopted grandmother."

This makes me smile widely and I suddenly feel better about snuggling into her before. She's not my mom, and it's nice to know that she's not trying to take my mom's spot. But I love the idea of a grandmother who lives nearby and who will bring me embroidered hankies and help me through tough times.

"Deal," I say, finally smiling at her. "Thanks, Mrs. Matthews. Now, shall we get on with the math?"

"I thought that you'd never ask!" Her voice is light and the small bit of laughter in it makes me smile. As I lead her to the kitchen, I can't help but think about what she said.

She's right: I don't need to carry this sadness for my dad. I can be sad with him, but he had nothing to do with these two men dying. I will have to remind myself that, but I have a pretty good feeling that Mrs. Matthews will help me remember if I ever forget. I love the idea that she wants to be a part of my life.

Summer math tutoring sounded awful when my dad first told me about it, but maybe it was just what I needed right now. Mrs. Matthews may have been my teacher during the school year, but we're not in school any longer. I've grown up and now I'm someone she wants to talk to and help, not just some lazy kid who didn't do the math homework.

CAROL

fter saying goodbye to Lilah on Monday, I knew
that I wanted to get her a little something for when
I went to visit her on Wednesday. That's why I have a book
tucked in my tote bag for her. It wasn't one that I owned,
because I'm not interested in actually giving her something
of mine, but rather one that I picked up for her.

The Joy of Cooking probably adds three pounds to my
tote bag, so I'll be more than happy to offload it, but I have a
pretty good feeling that it will make a great impression not
only on Lilah, but also her father. I haven't seen him since
our meeting at the cafe when I told him that Lilah needed
some tutoring.

There's always a check waiting for me when I get to
their house every morning to pay for my time there, so I
know that he's still aware that I'm coming around. Lilah has
mentioned before that he heads into work pretty early in
the morning so that he can stay on top of his case load, but I
still think that it's pretty weird that he doesn't want to be
around at least when I first arrive.

Wouldn't you want to know the person spending so

much time with your daughter? Maybe he's just happy that she's learning how to cook and will be a bit more helpful around the house from now on. He wouldn't be paying me at all if he knew the truth about what I was doing and why I wanted to be so close to Lilah, but there's no way that he'll ever find out.

I rap once on the front door and Lilah swings it open, a huge grin on her face. I shift my tote bag and reach inside, pulling the cookbook out and handing it to her.

"I thought that it was time for you to have something to flip through for inspiration," I say. "I figured that you could choose some recipes that you wanted to make and the two of us could work our way through them."

Lilah stares at me like she can't quite believe what I'm saying, then she breaks into an even bigger smile. "Really? Are you serious right now?"

When I nod, she beams, clutching the book to her chest and swaying back and forth happily before stepping aside so I can come into the house. I move past her, not waiting for her to invite me in. We've been doing this for over a week now, and I'm already feeling quite at home.

A girl could get used to a house like this. It's obvious from the art on the walls and the incredible wide plank wood floors that Grey hasn't spared any expense with the place. It's gorgeous, with furniture that looks expensive.

Well, all except for that sofa. Every time I look at it I wrinkle my nose and try to pretend that I don't see it sitting there. Why a doctor—a cardiologist, no less—would want a ratty old piece of furniture like that is just beyond me. It's the first thing that I would get rid of.

"Are you ready for some math?" I ask Lilah, who has already pulled out a seat at the kitchen table and is sitting, waiting. When she gives me a nod, I slip some worksheets from my bag. She's an eager student, although I'm pretty sure that the only reason she's trying so hard is because she wants to get straight to cooking.

$$\sim$$

*B*y the time I leave Lilah, it's well past lunch. Trent called me twice right around noon to find out where I was, but I didn't pick up either time. He can fend for himself for a change. I'm sure that he's more than capable of making a sandwich, and the absolute last thing that I wanted to do was rush home to him.

By the time I leave, though, I'm more than ready to go home and put my feet up. All of this standing and working in the kitchen is wearing me out.

"Remember," I say to Lilah, who's come out to the front porch to wave goodbye, "make sure that you clean up the kitchen completely or I'm sure that your dad will have a fit about just how many cookies we made."

The Bennetts have the best of everything, including the highest quality chocolate chips that I simply can't afford to buy. It's not that Trent didn't make good money before he retired, but the medical bills for George's surgery have chased me all of my adult life. It's the only reason why I'm still teaching.

I'm much more cut out for living in the lap of luxury.

Lilah closes the door after waving goodbye one more time. Even though I know that my little beater car probably draws attention simply by being parked in this neighborhood and I should pull away, I sit there for a moment and just look at the house. The houses all look similar, with rock facades and huge front porches, but each one has been designed to be just a little bit different than the others.

The Bennetts' house has a huge second story balcony across the front. When I asked Lilah about it she told me that it was off her dad's room. I've always wanted a balcony like that. Being able to drink my coffee up there in the morning while everyone else in the neighborhood scurried off to work sounds like heaven.

Their house also has a huge flower garden taking up half of the front yard. I can't exactly see Dr. Bennett out there getting his precious hands in the dirt, so they must have a gardener who comes sometimes when I'm not around. I'd be more than happy to keep the gardener on, especially if it meant that the house could look like that without me having to do any of the work.

All in all, I can only imagine how happy I'd be living in this house. It's not the one that I would pick for myself if I drove past it, but there's really nothing wrong with it. It's just a shame that it's so big and that I'm too old to fill it with children.

That was something that George and I had wanted but hadn't been able to do. Having lots of kids in a house like this would make it perfect. If I squint, I can just imagine them coming downstairs early in the morning for breakfast, all of us sitting on the front porch in the late afternoons, reading or talking.

My life was going to be amazing. I knew exactly what I wanted from it and how I wanted it to go. George and I were going to be so happy together.

But then Dr. Bennett took everything from me and it all came to a screeching halt.

I don't even realize that I'm gripping the steering wheel as tightly as I am until I hear the sound of the faux leather squeaking a little bit under my grip. Immediately, I force myself to relax my grip and take some deep calming breaths. Ocean Breath, they call it in yoga class.

It's okay. My life may not have worked out the way that I wanted it to up to this point, but there's no reason why I can't take control of it now and turn it around. There's no reason why I can't get what I deserve now.

Get back what was taken from me.

My phone rings again and I can't help but roll my eyes when I see that it's Trent calling yet again. I have to bite my tongue to keep from snapping at him when I pick up.

"Hey, darling," he says, and I feel my back stiffen a touch at his words. "Do you think that you're going to be home anytime soon? I'm really hungry."

"You haven't made yourself lunch?" It's so stupid that he can't do these things on his own, and I can't believe that he didn't just handle it while I was gone. "You've been waiting on me this entire time?"

He chuckles. "Of course I have! You're my wife. What, did you think that I'd ever want to do anything without you?"

Yes. That's exactly what I thought. I'd never tell him, but the one part of my life that I'm really looking forward to in the future is not having him around any longer. I want nothing to do with him anymore.

Forcing a smile in the hopes it seeps into my voice, I start the car and finally pull away from the curb. "Well," I say, trying to keep my voice as light and happy as possible, "I'm on my way now, so don't you worry." Before he has a chance to respond, I hang up, then toss my phone onto the passenger seat. It bounces once and falls to the floor, but I don't care.

I don't need it right now. All I have to do is keep working on my plan.

GREY

*E*arly Saturday morning is the perfect time to pound the pavement after a long week, and loud music pumps through the new earbuds that I bought myself last weekend. I ordered them with one-click before I'd really had time to consider whether or not I needed them, but now that I'm using them, I can see that yeah, I did.

I like to treat myself once in a while. I don't like to do it too often because I'm busy stashing money away for Lilah to go to college, but buying yourself a treat from time to time is the best way to keep from going insane. Of course, I felt a twinge of guilt about how much they cost, so when they arrived last night I immediately transferred the same amount to a local charity.

Sara always did that. At first I thought it was a little odd, but over time, I started to do it, too. Any large purchases were immediately matched with a donation of the same amount to a local charity. She told me that she knew how blessed the two of us were and that it didn't feel right to her to hoard everything to herself.

So blessed, I think bitterly, *that she died well before she should have.*

It wasn't until after her funeral that I took up running. At first I couldn't even make it all the way around the block without giving up and walking the rest of the way, but I kept pushing myself. There's nothing like the death of a spouse to make you stare your own mortality straight in the eye and wonder how much longer you really have left.

And since I was suddenly in charge of keeping Lilah safe, I had to do something. I couldn't simply be the cardiologist who saved people's lives without doing something to keep myself healthy as well.

As I run, I shake my head, trying to clear it. It's one thing to lose a patient years after you've done the surgery. Life happens, and no matter how great the heart that you give someone is, it will eventually fail. We all know this. We talked about it during my residency, how you can do everything right and you'll still lose patients.

But we didn't talk about losing two in two weeks.

It's not on the news anymore, which is great, because seeing my patients' faces plastered all over the TV screen after their deaths had been really hard for me. It was terrible to see two men I knew from operating on them and then to imagine them dead.

I did everything that I could to give them the best shot at life, and it still didn't matter.

"What am I doing?" I ask, stopping on the sidewalk and bending over to grab my thighs. My head pounds because I stopped so suddenly and I close my eyes, breathing deeply, trying to clear away the pressure in my temples.

"Dad?" Lilah's voice, slightly wobbly, cuts through my thoughts and I straighten up, blinking hard at her. I hadn't realized that I had stopped right in front of our house. If she hadn't come out to talk to me, I probably would have kept on running for another hour or so.

"Hey, honey. You okay?" Quickly, I scan her face. Her face is a little drawn. Something's bothering her, something that's happened since I peeked in on her to make sure she was still asleep before I left the house for my run.

She waits for a car to drive past. Mr. Lange, who lives down the street, taps his horn lightly in greeting before zipping on.

"Dad, I need you to come in." Her voice trembles a little bit and I grab her arms, squeezing them as I stare at her.

"What's wrong? Are you hurt, Lilah? What happened?" She looks physically okay, perfectly healthy, she just has an expression on her face that has me concerned. "Tell me what happened," I repeat.

A shake of her head and she chews on her lower lip, which is what she always does when she's really stressed out about something. It's been her tell for as long as I can remember.

"Please, just come into the house," she says, grabbing my hand and tugging me up the sidewalk. "There's something that you have to see, Dad. Come on. Please."

There's a note of panic in her voice and I finally follow her, putting one foot carefully in front of the other. I'd felt free running just a bit ago, but now I feel like I'm walking through molasses, it's so difficult to make my body do what I want it to.

Once inside, she shuts and locks the door, then points at the TV.

It's on, but the volume is turned way down, and I grab the remote, mashing down the volume button so that I can actually hear it.

"...police aren't entirely sure when Mr. Bert Pierce died,

75

but they do know one thing—he was not dressed to be out in his yard late at night. The entire neighborhood is in mourning, of course, and the shock is sure to ripple out from that community and touch everyone in town." The perky blonde stares right into the camera as she speaks like she's auditioning for some reality show.

"What is this?" Without realizing what I'm doing, I sink into a chair and stare at the screen. "Lilah?"

"It's all they're talking about this morning." She sinks onto the sofa, curling her legs up underneath her and tugging them close to her chest. I suddenly realize that she's still in her pajamas. Sitting there like that, she looks so much like her mother that I have to look away.

"I know him." The words are sand in my mouth. "I did his heart a few years ago."

She nods. "I know. That's why I wanted you to come in here as quickly as possible." A slight pause and her eyes flick to me like she's trying to gauge my reaction to what she's going to say. "That's three of your patients, dad. What do you think is going on?"

I don't know how to answer her because I have no idea what's happening. My head spins and I want to turn off the TV so that I don't have to hear what else they're saying, but just lifting the remote seems like an impossible task.

"I have no idea." I look from the TV to my daughter. "Is someone killing my patients?"

She gives her head a little shake right as the doorbell rings. Lilah's eyes widen and she unfolds from the sofa, obviously going to answer the door, but I hold up my hand.

"You sit," I tell her. "Or go change, if you want. I've got this."

Adrenaline pumps through my body as I walk to the

door. One glance through the peephole tells me that I have to open it, no matter if I want to or not.

GREY

*a*t first glance, the officer standing on my front porch looks completely new to law enforcement. She has scrubbed cheeks that make her look almost as young as my daughter and her hair is pulled back in a ponytail that's so tight that if she did have any lines around her eyes, they'd be pulled away in a skinny minute.

As soon as I open the door, however, I feel her gaze sweep over me, sizing me up, and I realize that I was completely wrong about her. She looks young, but from the way she's scanning me, like she's logging all of the information about me that she'll ever need, she's obviously been at this for a while.

"Dr. Bennett?" she asks, her eyes flicking up to my face, and I nod. "Good morning, I'm Detective Laite. Do you have a moment for us to talk right now?"

I'm still sweating terribly from my run and want nothing more than a cup of coffee to help clear my head and make it easier for me to think, but I know that there's no way that I can shut the door on the detective and not have it come back to bite me later, so I step aside, a smile on my face, to let her in.

"I'm about to make some coffee after my morning run," I tell her. "Would you like some?"

"This won't take that long." She positions herself in the middle of the living room and looks around like she's trying to determine what kind of person I am from the wall color and the stack of books on the coffee table. "Do you run every morning?"

"On the weekends I do," I tell her. "During the week it usually has to wait until after I get home from work."

A quick nod. "Have you seen the news this morning, doctor?"

She has to know that I have, since the TV is still turned to the news behind her. I gesture at it. "I just got in from my run and turned it on," I say. I know exactly where she's going with this, but part of me wants to have her lead the conversation. Even though I have a good idea of what she wants from me, I still want her to be the one to take us there.

"So you saw the news about your former patient, Bert Pierce?"

She cuts right to the chase, doesn't she? Swallowing hard, I nod. "I did. Terrible stuff."

"And I'm assuming that you also heard about your other two former patients who died, am I correct?"

"I did." From watching way too many crime documentaries, I know that even though I've done nothing wrong, the last thing that I want to do is start running my mouth. That never ends well, even if you are innocent.

"Then I assume that you know why I'm here," she says, pulling a notepad from her pocket. She clicks her pen half a dozen times then looks up at me. "It's just strange to some of us at the department that the only obvious connection that the three of them have is that you were their doctor. Have you seen or talked to any of the three men lately?"

Slowly, I shake my head, then I sit down in the same chair I was in before she came. My legs are tired from my run and the anxious feeling in my stomach isn't helping any. "Not lately, no. After a patient has a transplant, they do have to come back regularly for check-ups and to make sure that there isn't any chance of a rejection. After a while, though, the frequency of those checkups decreases dramatically and they have a more and more normal life."

I pause, thinking hard. "It's been a long time since those surgeries," I say, trying hard to remember. "It was strange, there was a handful of them at the same time, all local, but then my success with them helped draw more attention to the hospital, and they just kept coming."

"They?" She tilts her head at me, her pen poised from writing on her pad.

"People from out of town. Patients who heard about my success rate. But the three men who died, their surgeries were all a long time ago."

"Can you think of anyone in your office they might have all dealt with and had a problem with? A nurse, or a secretary perhaps, who would want to hurt them for some reason?"

I shake my head. "Not in the least. Everyone on staff understands that taking care of the patient and keeping them mentally healthy and strong is the best way to work towards a good outcome. Everyone's rooting for the patient, I can't remember there ever being any altercations or problems."

"Great. Thank you." She flips her pad shut and moves like she's going to put it back in her pocket before she stops and looks at me. "Before I forget, where were you last night?"

"Here. In bed." I pause, then the full reality of what she's asking crashes down on me. "You don't think that I'm a suspect, do you? You can't possibly think that I would ever hurt someone, especially an old patient?"

"I'm just covering all of my bases, sir. Is there anyone who can vouch for you being home last night?"

"I can." Lilah's voice makes the detective turn around and I look up, surprised to see her standing in the door. I wonder how long she's been listening, but the look on her face tells me everything.

She's heard enough to know why the detective is here.

"And you are his daughter?" The notepad gets flipped back open and she clicks the pen a few more times, like she has to prime it to get it to work.

"Yes. I'm Lilah. With an H on the end. My dad and I were here all last night. We made pizza together and then watched a movie before going to bed." She lifts her chin a little bit, like doing so is going to make the detective more inclined to believe her.

I want to go to my daughter and wrap my arms around her to protect her from what's happening right now, but I know better. Detective Laite is writing on her pad and only pauses long enough to ask one last question.

"Was he with you the past two weekends, as well?"

Lilah nods. "Of course he was. Since Mom died, it's always been just the two of us. Dad wouldn't hurt anyone, Detective. He saves lives, he's not exactly interested in taking them again later."

This makes the detective look up. She gazes at my daughter without speaking for so long that I finally stand, wondering if I need to intervene. "Thank you, Lilah."

Before my daughter can answer, she turns to me. "Sorry about the early morning interruption, Dr. Bennett. I hope that you and your daughter have a good rest of the weekend. If any other questions come up, I'll be back."

"Of course," I say. "I'll let you out." I take a step towards the door but she flaps her hand at me, shooing me away.

"I know how doors work, Dr. Bennett."

Lilah and I don't move until she's outside, then my daughter rushes to the window, pulling back the curtain just enough to peek out. When the detective is gone she turns, letting the curtain fall from her fingers.

"Dad?" Lilah's voice trembles. "Do they really think that you killed Mr. Pierce? Is that why she was here?"

I cross the room to my daughter and fold her into my arms, wondering how much longer she's going to let me do this now that she's growing up.

"They're just checking all the boxes," I tell her, squeezing her tight. "She said that the one connection that they could find between the three men is that they were all my patients years ago. It doesn't mean anything, darling. It just means that there are sometimes strange coincidences in the world that you simply can't explain away. I'm sorry you have to go through something like this. It's not fair."

She nods but doesn't pull away from me. After another moment, though, she takes a huge sniff and steps back. "You need to shower," she tells me, dramatically pinching her nose. "I don't think that I can eat anything with you stinking up the house."

I laugh, even though there's a huge leaden ball in my stomach making it difficult for me to breathe. "I'll shower, but only if you make us breakfast, and cereal doesn't count."

She pouts, still pinching her nose so that her voice

comes out higher than it should. "I thought that we could go to Main Street and get some waffles."

The last thing that I want to do right now is be recognized outside of my house. I'm sure that all of the neighbors got a good eyeful of the detective here and I can practically hear them all whispering about it. "Sorry, sweetheart, not today," I tell her. "Today is breakfast at home before I demolish you at chess."

This makes her grin. "Let's make a bet. I beat you at chess and you take me out for waffles tomorrow morning." She looks relentless, like there's no way that she's going to give up on this, so I nod.

"Fair, and when I destroy you, which I will, you also have to make lunch." I think for a moment that she's not going to agree, but then she gives me a swift nod and turns to the kitchen.

"Deal. Just get ready, Dad, because I heard that the waffles are extra good on Sunday morning. I can't wait."

She disappears into the kitchen and I grab onto the back of a chair for support. My heart pounds in my chest like I'm in the middle of a run and I have taken a hill too fast..

I don't know what's going on right now, but I can't get rid of this terrible sense of doom.

LILAH

I didn't get waffles for breakfast yesterday. Dad keeps telling me that I'm getting a lot better at chess, but he still pulls out all of the stops and can easily beat me when he really wants to. Of course, I kept up my end of the deal and made lunch, and then he surprised me by ordering take-out for dinner. The leftovers are in the fridge but I have a feeling that Carol will help me make something else to eat, so I shoved them to the back behind the eggs so that she didn't get the idea that I don't want her help any longer.

When she rings the doorbell I throw it open, then my eyes fly open in surprise. Instead of her usual khakis and sweater, today she has on khakis, hiking boots, and an outdoorsy shirt in a material that is designed to wick moisture away from the body.

"What, have you never seen someone dressed for an adventure before?" she asks, tilting her head to the side a little to look at me quizzically. "Probably not, now I that I think about it. You look like you're dressed for a Netflix marathon."

"I'm dressed for algebra tutoring and some cooking," I say, but she shakes her head.

"That's going to have to wait. I talked to your dad and told him that you're making such great progress that I wanted to take you somewhere special today and he agreed."

"There's no math today?" Excitement brews in me and I grin at her. "Seriously? He agreed to this?" When she nods, I shoot another question at her. "Where in the world are we going?"

"Go get changed and I'll show you. No leggings, Lilah. Put on some real pants, preferably without so many holes in them that I worry about them rotting off of you while we're out and about."

I grin at her and she steps into the house to wait. She closes the door and leans against it before flapping her hand at me impatiently. "Go. I have some worksheets in the car just in case of a math emergency and I will get them out if you don't move it."

"A math emergency?" I call over my shoulder as I run from the living room and bound up the stairs. This is awesome. Dad didn't mention that I'd have the morning off of tutoring, but to be fair, he was a little stressed out after the detective came by. I don't blame him.

It takes me a few minutes to find a pair of jeans that I'm sure will pass Mrs. Matthews' test about not falling to pieces and I pull them on before yanking on some sneakers and changing my shirt. She said that we're going on an adventure, so I put my hair up in a ponytail to keep it out of my face before running back downstairs.

She's right where I left her, leaning up against the door like it's her job to make sure that the house doesn't fall down around us. Her eyes flick over me and I see her give a quick nod, obviously approving of what I'm wearing.

"Look okay?" I ask her anxiously.

"Great. Glad to know that you have some clothes that don't look like rats chewed through them." Her words are harsh but I notice the smile at the corners of her mouth.

"It's called fashion," I retort, grabbing my purse and throwing it over my shoulder. "It's what all of the cool kids are wearing."

"Holy moley," she sighs as she steps outside and waits on the porch while I lock up the house. "Being a teenager looks so much harder now that it was in my day."

I nod, slipping my key back into my purse, then follow her to her car. "It's...well, let's just say that sometimes I wish I were homeschooled." I throw her a grin as I get into her car, then buckle up before really looking around.

Her car is perfectly clean. It honestly looks like she just bought it and drove it here from the dealer, except for the fact that it's probably as old as I am. I'm pretty sure that nobody has ever eaten anything in there. There isn't a single crumb on the mat on the floor, nor is there a speck of dust.

Most cars have *something* dirty in them, like a smeared window or fingerprints on the dash, but this car is perfect. Folding my hands, I put them in my lap, afraid to touch anything. It's not a nice car on the outside, that's for sure. I'm pretty sure that it's what my dad would call a beater, but on the inside you'd think that it was a Lexus or something, it's so clean.

Mrs. Matthews buckles up, seemingly oblivious to how I'm checking out her car, and we pull away from our house. "You've been working really hard on cooking," she says, "and you've actually come a long way. I told your dad that I thought it was time for you to go to the source."

"The source?" Her compliment about how well I've been doing made my chest swell, but I have no idea what kind of source she's talking about. "You're taking me to the grocery store?"

She laughs. "No, Lilah, not the grocery store. It's very interesting to me that your generation doesn't really know where your food comes from."

The way that she says it doesn't sound mean even though I'm sure that someone else saying the same thing to me would come across a little harsh. "So, a farm?"

"Closer. I grew up with survivalist parents." Glancing over, she must see the surprise on my face, because she grins and nods. "Yep. They firmly believed that the end of the world was coming soon and wanted to make sure that I'd be able to take care of myself when civilization collapsed."

My stomach twists. I've seen survivalist shows on Netflix with my dad. "Please tell me that we're not going to be hunting squirrels or something today. I honestly don't think that I could handle skinning one or anything like that."

Mrs. Matthews shakes her head. "No squirrels, no. We're going for a walk in the woods and I'm going to show you some edible plants that we have growing around here. It's pretty fun to forage for them yourself and then make a meal out of them."

Foraging for plants sounds much more bearable than hunting squirrels, and I feel myself relax a little bit. I still can't believe that my dad is okay with me blowing off math to go walk in the woods with my teacher and look for plants to eat, but I think he's just so stressed out about what's going on in the news that he doesn't care.

Honestly, he probably wouldn't even notice if I tried to serve him cold food for dinner. Instead of eating dinner and then watching a movie last night, which is what we normally do on Sunday, he ate and then retired to his study to read.

Read. Yeah, right. When I was getting ready for bed I crept down the hall and peeked in his door. He wasn't sitting in his comfy leather chair reading. There wasn't even a book open on it like he'd been reading and just decided to call it quits for the night. No, he'd been hunched over his computer, the eerie glow from the screen shining right on his face.

I have no way of knowing for sure what he was looking at, but I have a really good feeling that he was reading the news from the past few weeks. As far as I know, they still have no idea who has killed these three men.

I guess if it were just one person or the circumstances on the first death weren't so weird, they wouldn't really look into it. Three people dying one right after another, though? That's concerning.

"We're here," Mrs. Matthews announces, her voice cutting through my thoughts and bringing me back to my foraging expedition.

"I've come here before," I say, almost pressing my hand up against the window as I look out. It's only when I remember how clean her car is and that she'd probably hate me for leaving fingerprints on the glass that I restrain myself. "We used to come hiking here when I was younger, but I don't think that I've been here in years."

"Well, it's a great place for a beginner," she says, getting out of the car. I follow suit, tucking my phone into my pocket and leaving my purse underneath the seat. She stretches, reaching her hands high above her head before bending over and touching her toes before turning to look at me. I don't even know if I could do that. "You ready to find your lunch?"

A thrill of excitement runs through me. I never thought that I'd have this much fun with her. Mrs. Matthews is much cooler than I ever realized and I can't believe how much I'm learning from her.

"I'm ready. Got my hiking boots on and my most respectable jeans." This makes her laugh and I feel another swell of pride. I want to make her happy and enjoy spending time with me. She's the first person outside of my dad to seem to care about me and want to get to know me better.

I'm pretty sure that my mom would approve.

"Let's go, then," she says, nodding at the trailhead. "But stay alert, you never know what dangers you might run into in the woods."

CAROL

*L*ilah steps carefully through the woods, scanning back and forth on the trail in front of her as she looks for the plant I pointed out in my book. I'd told her that the easiest ones to find were the berry bushes, but that we wouldn't see any of those right here by the trailhead because most of them would be picked clean.

That's the problem with people now. They want everything to come easily to them and just skim from the top without actually working hard for anything. That's not how I was raised, and I'm certainly not going to change now.

"Remind me again what this is called?" Lilah says, slowing down to look over her shoulder at me.

"Wood sorrel. Remember, you can eat the tubers, but not the leaves or the flowers, so it's important always to be careful."

"Right." She turns the small trowel I gave her over and over in her hand before pointing off the trail a little bit. "There. That's wood sorrel, isn't it?"

"Excellent. Sure is. And what's that next to it?"

"Broadleaf plantain," she says confidently. When I nod

at her, she steps off of the trail to dig up the tubers. I have a small sack over my shoulder that's already brimming with food we've harvested, and when she returns, she carefully tucks the plants in. "Do you think that we have enough now?"

"Yes, unless you want to try for some berries." I point past her up the trail to where it cuts hard to the right around a large oak tree. "If I remember correctly, the trail goes through a swampy area right there that discourages most people from continuing. I'd imagine that we'd have some berries to eat in just a few minutes if we forge ahead. Also, there's a great overlook up there. I know that you've been wanting to see some good views."

This perks her right up. We've been in the woods for a long time now and her ponytail, once pert and bouncy, now hangs limp and tired on her back. "I'd love a good view," she says, turning and looking at the trail ahead. "Let's do it."

"Good girl," I say, following her. Lilah walks with renewed purpose now, really swinging her arms like that's going to help push her up the mountain faster. I keep up easily. When I'm not teaching or working on my plan then I'm out here in the woods, hiking and remembering all of the things that I learned when I was younger.

I've used some of those skills on the three men I've killed so far. I have no doubt in my mind that I won't ever be caught. Going to jail isn't part of the plan. I'll do anything in my power to keep from ruining my life like that.

Lilah works her way through the mud like a champ, carefully stepping on rocks and bits of bark to keep from sinking too deep into it. Even so, her hiking boots are going to be in rough shape when I drop her back off at home. I cringe at the thought of those muddy boots in my car. I wish I had some paper to put down.

It certainly isn't the nicest vehicle in town, but I do pride myself on making sure that it's clean and in good condition. Just because I can't afford an expensive car doesn't mean that I need to drive around a dirty piece of junk.

"Berries!" Lilah cries, running up the steep incline in front of her. I follow her quickly, not even breathing hard as we crest the top of the mountain and look down over the ridge.

Below and in front of us, the mountains and trees seem to stretch on forever. It's beautiful. Everything is a slightly different shade of dark green. The sky is impossibly blue and bright and we watch as an eagle wheels its way across the sky. The ground that we're standing on slants down slightly, and Lilah carefully picks her way closer to the edge of the overlook, wanting to see farther out.

Berry bushes surround us, most of them blueberry, and I pop one in my mouth, crushing it between my teeth as I watch her. She's almost too close to the edge now and I should call her back, but I just want to see what she's going to do. Part of me itches to walk up behind her and give her the gentlest nudge.

It wouldn't take much of anything to send her over the edge. It's so tempting.

Instead I grab another blueberry, crushing it between my fingers before I drop it to the ground.

"Careful by the edge," I call, and Lilah shuffles back a little bit. She's popping blueberries in her mouth as quickly as she can.

I want to take everything from Grey Bennett. I want to leave him a broken shell of a man, just as broken as I was after my George died. Even though I could speed up the timeline and take Lilah from him right here and right now, that's not going to do me any good. It's better that I wait until he's so far gone that there isn't any way that he can come back from the hell I've made of his life.

Part of me wants to push Grey Bennett so far that he ends it himself, but as beautifully satisfying as that would be, I think that there could actually be a much better outcome. Rather than letting him escape the horrors that his life is going to hold for him, I want him to stay alive.

I want him to watch as he loses everything that he holds dear. I'll take his sanity, his money, his house.

And then I'll take his daughter.

GREY

*T*he page over the hospital intercom stops me in my tracks. It's only Wednesday but it feels like this week has stretched on for months already. I'm on my way to get something to eat, not because I'm really hungry, but because I know that I need to continue to fuel myself if I'm going to make it through the rest of the day.

The only things that I see when I close my eyes are the faces of my three dead patients. Of course, I would never harm anyone, especially not someone whose life I'd already saved, but I saw the way Detective Laite looked at me when she came to talk to me at our house, like she was trying to see if she could believe me or not.

I know that she said that I'm the common link between the three men. They were all my patients and now, years later and for no apparent reason, they're all dead.

It makes no sense. I know that. Lilah knows that. All I can do is hope that the detectives all come to believe that, too.

The page comes again and I stop dead in my tracks, looking up at the speaker on the wall. They're placed every fifty feet or so along corridors and inside staff break rooms to make sure that when you're needed, you can be found immediately.

"Dr. Bennett to the front office, Dr. Bennett to the front office."

It's purposefully vague. Whenever the secretary pages someone, she always does it in a way that nobody can guess who's looking for them. It could be a phone call, a package, or, in my case, a visit from the local detective.

I just know that I'm going to turn the corner and see Detective Laite standing there.

"I'll walk with you, since you seem to have forgotten the way."

I turn at the voice coming from behind me and smile. Cherry. She's dressed in scrubs, just like I am, but is munching on a sandwich. When she sees my eyes flick to it, she rolls her eyes and hands me half.

"You're like a stray dog, you know that? Wandering around without a collar, trying to get food from anyone you can. Didn't Lilah pack you something to eat?"

She knows that Lilah and Mrs. Matthews have been making sure between them that I have something to eat every day. Gratefully, I take the sandwich and enjoy a huge bite, chewing and swallowing before I answer. "There weren't any leftovers last night, it was that good. So, yeah, she keeps me fed, but if I'd tried to get that last piece of chicken piccata from her last night she might have stabbed me with the fork."

"A girl after my own heart." Cherry starts walking, obviously expecting me to join her. I do, knowing full well that the longer I wait to go, the more likely it will be that I get paged again. "So, who's coming to visit you today? Do you have a secret admirer that you haven't told me about?"

I scoff. "Hardly. I think I told you that there was a detective at the house on Sunday, after the third one of my patients showed up dead?" My voice is low, barely above a whisper, just in case we pass a patient or a patient's family member. The last thing that they need is to hear doctors talking about dead patients.

She nods and takes another bite. "Mmm, yeah, but I thought that you said that was all taken care of."

Shrugging, I fall silent for a moment. I thought that it was all taken care of, too. I honestly can't see how anyone could possibly think that I'd have anything to do with a murder, let alone three. And to be fair, I don't know yet who wants to see me in the front office, but I have a really good feeling that it's going to be the detective.

"I'm not sure that it will really all be taken care of until they found whoever killed them," I say. "It doesn't exactly look good on the town to have three murders like that, back-to-back, does it? We all know that tourism is king here, especially during the summer."

"Good point. Have you thought about doing an investigation of your own? Seeing if you can beat them to the chase?"

Laughing, I turn the corner to the front office. "You know as well as I do that that only happens in books and movies. Nobody ever catches the killer on their own."

"They do when they're the next on the hit list." Cherry wiggles her eyebrows at me and I sigh, turning away. "I'm sorry, Grey," she says, the smile vanishing from her face as she grabs my arm so that I can't walk away from her. "I know that this is serious, I really do. You know me. I handle serious situations differently than most people do."

"I know. It's okay." I run my hand through my hair and she drops my arm. "I just can't help but worry that...well, I watch a lot of movies, and there's always some where the good guy gets screwed."

"Sure, but like you just said, that's just a movie. This is real life. Our cops aren't totally bumbling around in the dark without a clue, Grey, and it's obvious that you don't have a murderous bone in your body. If that is the detective, which you still don't know if it is, she probably just wants to tell you that she's cleared you and that she's sorry for upsetting you and wasting your time."

I know that my friend is probably wrong, but I also know that arguing about it won't solve anything. The only thing left for me to do is to go into the office and see what's waiting there for me. I give Cherry a smile then turn, opening the door and stepping through before allowing myself to look up at who's waiting there for me.

"Dr. Benett," Detective Laite says, her voice sounding falsely cheery, "I was just beginning to wonder if I'd have to have you paged again. You're a very busy man, I take it."

"Sorry for the delay." There's no reason to be rude to her or to take the bait that she's dangling right in front of my face. "I was getting lunch and the cafeteria can be a bit of a zoo this time of day."

"I see." She gives me a smile that doesn't quite reach her eyes and I sit down across from her when she gestures at the empty chair. "Well, I had some time to look through some more facts of the cases and wanted to run some stuff by you."

It's taking all of my self-control not to ask her if I'm under arrest, but I'm not sure if that's something that innocent or guilty people ask, so I swallow the question back and wait for her to continue.

"Toxicology reports aren't back on Mr. Pierce yet. There's a bit of a backlog right now, but we finally got the one back on the first victim, Mr. Ross. Looks like he wasn't totally in his right mind when he was out in the woods at night and then got trapped in the waterfall."

I want to reply tartly that nobody in their right mind would be out in the woods after dark wearing a full suit and dress shoes like he had been, but again I just wait for her to continue. I have a feeling that waiting to see what she's going to say is a good idea.

"It wasn't alcohol in his system, which surprised me. Honestly, I'd thought that he would have had to have been drunk to be out there in the woods dressed like that. It was something else."

She's baiting me, waiting to see what I'm going to say to her, but I have nothing to say. I didn't kill the three men, and she's not going to be able to blame the murders on me. When I don't budge and remain silent yet again, Detective Laite frowns a little and then drops the bomb that she's been holding onto.

"We're very lucky that his wife pushed for every test known to man to be done on her husband. I'm talking blood, urine, even hair tests. They're all very expensive, and some of them so new that I didn't even know that they existed. Luckily for us, his wife's brother works in rehab and knows some of the stranger substances to test for. I hate to admit it, but there are things out there that I didn't even know people took to get high."

"He was on drugs?" My curiosity is getting the better of me even though I'm trying my best to hold back from saying anything.

"Sure was." She sets her elbows on the table and leans across it to look at me. "Some of the things that we tested for are drugs extracted from plants. Ones that you can chew or smoke. Ever heard of salvia?"

I shake my head. "Never. What is it?"

"It's a pretty little plant with a purple flower, and believe me, Dr. Bennett, I could tell you all about this plant now, since I spent yesterday learning everything that I can about it. Unfortunately, pretty as it is, it also packs a potent little punch. It's really commonly grown in gardens because it's so attractive, so guess where my partner is right now."

My stomach drops. "I've never heard of it, never seen it," I tell her, "and I know for a fact that there isn't any in my garden."

"We'll see, won't we?" She leans back in her chair and smiles at me. "If you have a patient to attend to, doctor, don't let me keep you. I'll know where to find you if my partner turns anything up."

LILAH

*M*rs. Matthews has just left, wiggling her fingers at me as she gets into her car to drive off. I wave goodbye from the door and then lock it, shutting myself in the house. It was so cool on Monday, walking through the woods with her and learning about local plants, that it was almost a let-down to be back in the house doing math and learning about cooking today.

I'd never known that spending time outside could be so fun, or so delicious. There's still a plastic cup with some blueberries in the fridge and I'm going to make some blueberry muffins this afternoon as a treat for my dad. That's one thing that I remember my mom making all the time when I was younger. I'm not sure how mine will turn out, but if they're terrible I can always just throw them away and he'll never know.

The sound of a car in the driveway stops me from going into the kitchen. Mrs. Matthews must have forgotten something and I open the door up again, a smile on my face.

But it isn't her little beater sitting in the driveway. It's a sleek black car with heavily tinted windows, and I stare at it as the door slowly opens. Even though I have no reason to be scared, the fact that I don't know who's in the vehicle makes me nervous and I grip the door frame hard, digging my nails hard into the wood.

A tall man I've never seen before emerges from the car and pauses, looking around for a moment like he's making sure that he has the right place before he shuts his door and glances up at the house. I know that he sees me because he somehow manages a smile, even though I have a feeling that he doesn't really mean it.

"Lilah Bennett?" he calls, still standing by his car. I give him a swift nod but don't answer, and he starts up the sidewalk towards me, pulling a business card from his pocket. "I'm Detective Tanner, Detective Laite's partner. She wanted me to come by and check on some things."

"My dad's not home," I say, taking the card from him. "So I don't know what you want me to do…" Ugh, I wish more than anything that Mrs. Matthews was still here. She's savvy and would know what to say to the detective and how to make me feel better.

"I don't need to talk to your dad, Lilah, don't worry. In fact, he knows that I'm coming by because my partner is meeting with him now. I'm just here to look around the house for a few things."

My heart slams hard in my chest but I swallow down the fear threatening to choke me. "Is there anything that I can do to help?"

"Nope, I'm fine." This time when he smiles at me it looks more genuine and I relax some. I still don't know why he's here or what he's doing, but the fact that he doesn't need anything from me makes me feel a lot better.

"Can you tell me what you're looking for?" I'll bet that the sooner he finishes up here, the sooner he'll leave. I want to see him go so that I can call my dad and check in with him. "I might be able to point you in the right direction."

I see the indecision on his face. It's obvious that he doesn't want to ask me for help but that he would love to be done with this job as soon as possible. "Don't worry about it, Lilah. You just go on inside and enjoy the rest of your day. I'll be out of your way soon enough, okay?"

Even though I feel like I should stick with him and try to keep an eye on what he's doing, I shut the door anyway and lock it up tight. My heart is pounding as I run to get my cell phone from the charger in the kitchen. When I dial my dad, he doesn't pick up. I'm used to it going straight to voicemail when he's working, but I still swear in frustration when I hang up the phone.

For a moment, I feel stuck. I don't know what to do, but I do know that I need to do something. I turn my phone over in my hand a few times before I take a deep breath and dial Mrs. Matthews. She picks up on the first ring and a wave of gratitude sweeps over me. It's so powerful that I actually grab the kitchen counter to keep from falling over.

"Mrs. Matthews, it's Lilah. A detective is here looking around the yard and my dad's still not home and I don't know what to do." The words spill out of me like a dam has burst and I hear her suck in a breath when I finish speaking.

"Your dad isn't home?" She asks. I hear a horn honking in the distance, so I know that she's still driving, but I have no idea where she was going after this.

"No," I say, shaking my head even though she can't see me. "And I called him but he didn't pick up." I don't tell her that I feel like I'm going to be sick or that my palms are sweaty. I don't mention the fact that I'm honestly scared about having this guy out in the yard poking around.

It's not like he's going to find anything, but just the

thought of him out there looking hard for some evidence that could hurt my dad is enough to make me feel sick.

"I'm turning around, Lilah. Did he show you a badge? Do you know for sure that he's a real detective and not just someone trying to get into the house?"

I feel icy fingers of fear grip the back of my neck. That thought had never occurred to me. Why didn't I ask him for his badge to prove who he was? "He gave me his business card," I say weakly, knowing full well that it's easy enough to go online and order business card that say whatever you want them to. How could I be so stupid?

"Got it. Don't worry, I'm sure he's legit, I just want you to be safe." Her words are bright and crisp. "Now, Lilah, I can stay on the phone with you if you want while I drive back, or I'll be there in just a few minutes. I'm not very far away from your house."

"I don't need you to stay on the phone," I say, suddenly feeling silly. It's not like I'm a little kid who's afraid of being left home alone, and it's not like he's done or said anything threatening. I just don't like that he's here on our property and my dad isn't.

"Okay. Hang tight, darling." Mrs. Matthews hangs up and I go to the front window, carefully lifting the curtain so that I can peer out.

The detective is in the garden, slowly walking among the plants. He has a picture in one hand and keeps referring to it as he looks at the different things growing and blooming. Most of our neighbors have stopped at one time or another to tell us how much they love our garden, but I know without a doubt that that's not what Detective Tanner is doing.

He's looking for something.

The thought that he honestly thinks that my dad could

have anything to do with the three murders makes me feel sick to my stomach, even though I know my dad is innocent and no matter what the detective is looking for, he could look for days and not find any evidence.

As I'm staring at him, trying to see what's on the picture in his hand, Mrs. Matthews pulls back into the driveway. Unlike the detective, who sat in his car for a second to get his bearings before getting out, she's out the door in a flash, marching right up to him. I move quickly away from the window, throwing open the front door to join her.

She makes me feel brave. It doesn't matter what happens right now because I know that I have her on my side and she'll take care of whatever's going to happen. Behind me, I hear my phone ring and I hesitate. I'm sure that it's my dad and I should probably pick it up, but I need to know what's going on out here first.

I close the door firmly behind me, cutting off the sound of my phone.

"Hello," Mrs. Matthews calls, marching right up to the detective. She's not very tall but has pulled herself up as tall as she can go before she gives him a once-over, staring hard at the badge on his hip before glancing at the gun and hand-cuffs on his duty belt. "Can I help you?"

She sounds so brave and tough that I can't help the smile on my face. She'll take care of this, whatever this is, I know she will. For the first time since he showed up, I'm not scared.

CAROL

*L*ilah called me for help.

That makes me so happy that I could scream, but I manage to keep my face perfectly impassive when talking to the detective who is currently standing in the middle of the Bennett garden. He's up to his waist in flowers and looking at me like he's never seen anyone he hates quite as much.

That's fine. I know that it's not personal and that he would just rather be doing anything else than looking for something in the garden. My heart beats a little faster when I see that he has a picture of a plant in his hand and I try to get a look at what it is, but he twists his wrist a little, angling his notebook away from me.

They couldn't possibly have figured out about the salvia already, could they? I honestly thought that that little trick would keep them busy for months.

Who knew that someone in toxicology on the little police force right here in the mountains of Tennessee would be so clever?

"I'm sorry, and who are you?" He doesn't look sorry at

all. Rather, he looks hot, tired and irritated, and like he's already thinking about the beer that his wife will have waiting for him when he gets off work. I glance down at his left hand and spot a gold band there, confirming my thoughts.

"I'm Mrs. Carol Matthews," I say, walking through the garden to force him to shake my hand. "I'm a friend of Lilah's. She was a little unclear about what you were doing here and called me to make sure that everything is okay."

"Detective Tanner. Everything's fine, ma'am, just getting some information out here."

"Do you mind if I see your badge?" I ask, even though it's in plain sight.

"I'm sorry." He looks confused. "You want to see my badge?"

I nod, really playing it up for Lilah. She needs to see that I'm on her side and that she can trust me. It's not a bad idea for this detective to know I'm willing to go to bat for her, either. It'll make it that much easier when I step up to take guardianship of Lilah.

"Just to make sure that you are who you say you are," I tell him, smiling at him. When he doesn't move, I lean forward, dropping my voice a little. "You scared Lilah," I whisper. "I'm sorry, I know that you're legit, but I promised her that I'd come by and just make sure that everything is above water here."

"Oh, I understand," he murmurs, then unclips his badge and hands it to me. "Didn't realize that that's what was going on."

I run my fingers over it and put on a good show of really checking it out before handing it back over. "Thank you," I whisper, then raise my voice again. "And what exactly are you looking for here? How can we help you speed this process up a little bit?"

"Don't you worry about me," he says. "If you want to be helpful, take Lilah in, get her some tea. She doesn't look too chipper." Then he turns from me and starts working his way through the garden again.

This makes me glance over at the porch. Lilah's staring at the two of us like she isn't quite sure that she can believe what she's seeing. She looks nervous and I'd feel bad for her if it weren't for the fact that her father ruined my life. Poor girl didn't do anything to deserve having a monster like that for her father.

It's a kindness, really, what I'm doing. No child should have to live with a parent who is evil, and that's exactly what Lilah has had to do for her entire life. Even though I know that I need Dr. Bennett to be held accountable for what he did to me and to George, part of me also knows that I'm doing this for Lilah.

I'm going to save her from this terrible life with a father who can't possibly love her. She won't be able to see it now, but I'm giving her a gift and I'm sure that she'll recognize that later, when she's a little older.

I pick my way quickly through the daisies and peonies, walking up to the porch to greet her.

"Well?" She asks, picking at the hem of her shirt. "Did you find out what he's looking for? Is he legit? Do I need to worry about him being here?"

I put my arm over her shoulder and direct her back to the house. She doesn't want to go inside with me but I'm stronger than her and I keep my arm tight around her back until she relents and opens the door. Once inside, I lead her straight into the kitchen and then point her to a stool, walking over to the cupboards to get some tea.

At first, I'd been a little daunted by the size of their kitchen. It was clearly designed for throwing huge dinner parties and it took me a little while to get used to the layout and where everything was kept. Now that I've been in here so much, though, I'm feeling more and more at home. I know right where the tea is and I pull it down before putting a kettle of water on the stove to heat up.

Lilah likes her tea with honey and I grab the bear of local organic honey, squeezing a bit into her cup before pulling out the milk. By the time the water is warm I have the tea bags in the mugs—earl grey for her, chamomile for me—and plunk hers down in front of her so it can steep.

"There," I say, sitting down next to her and rubbing her back, "you'll feel a bit better after you get some nice warm tea in you, Lilah. I swear, there are very few things in this world that a cup of tea and time with someone who cares can't fix."

She reaches out and wraps her hands around her mug before giving me a thin smile. "Do they really think that dad could have had something to do with the murders? I just don't see how that could possibly be. He saves people, he doesn't kill them...and why in the world would he want to hurt a patient after he already saved their life? It makes no sense."

I'm a master at keeping emotion out of my face, so I'm sure that Lilah has no idea how much disgust is coursing through me right now. Of course, she'd think that her dad was the hero in this story. He's got her brainwashed into believing that he can do no wrong. She honestly sees him as the knight in shining armor coming to save the day and to heal people.

She has no idea what he did to me. He's not the hero here, he's the villain. He's evil, pure evil, and it's up to me to stop him. Someone has to, and I'm the only person who's brave enough to take on that challenge.

"I have no idea, darling," I say, rubbing her shoulder. She leans towards me a little for comfort and I give her a squeeze. "I think that they're just covering all of their bases so that when they do finally find the murderer that they can be sure that they looked at this from every angle. They don't only gather evidence to convict people. Sometimes they use it to rule someone out."

I have no idea if that's true or not, but it sounds good, and Lilah seems to buy it. She nods and chews on her lower lip like she's really thinking about what I just said before she sits up a bit straighter and nods again, a bit more definitely this time.

"Okay. Yeah. That makes sense. Just because he's here doesn't mean that he wants to find evidence against my dad. He could be looking for something that will prove my dad is innocent." She gives me a smile. "Thanks, Mrs. Matthews. I knew that calling you was the right thing to do."

I'm about to tell her that I'm so glad she called me so that I could support her right now when her phone rings. Lilah jumps from her seat and darts across the kitchen for it. "My dad," she says, holding it up to show me the screen. "He called me back but I missed it and I forgot to return his call. I have to take this."

"Of course you do, darling," I say, taking a sip of my tea. It's still a little hot, but I don't care. I wouldn't miss this conversation for the world.

GREY

"*D*ad?"

Lilah sounds scared and I bend over, resting my palm on my office wall. I honestly feel like I need something strong to support me when I hear how worried she is. I missed her call and tried to call her back a moment later, but she didn't pick up. Now, hearing her voice, I feel a flood of emotions.

Worry, mainly, because I know that she has to be nervous to have a detective wandering around outside our house. She also sounds tired, like she wants to go to bed. Lastly, there's a touch of anger in her voice, a new accusatory tone that I wish wasn't there.

"Lilah, are you okay?" I want to go home to her, but I have a stent to put in this afternoon. There's just no way that I can reschedule a surgery like that no matter how much I'd like to. I hate the idea of leaving Lilah alone when she's so incredibly worried, but I don't have the type of job that I can just walk away from.

Lilah knows that. It's never been an issue before. As

much as I'd like to leave right now to be home with her, I have to be here. She has to be there. She gets that.

My fingers grip the phone so tightly that I'm afraid that the screen is going to crack. I feel stress at the back of my neck and I inhale deeply, remembering the breathing exercises that my therapist taught me after Sara died.

Some days I hated having to do them. I hated focusing on my breath when Sara didn't have any breath at all in her body. I found it ironic that I struggled to breathe when she wouldn't ever get the chance to do so again. It wasn't fair.

It still isn't fair.

"I'm okay, Dad" she says after a pause. "I called Mrs. Matthews and she came right over. She checked the detective's badge to make sure that he was who he said he was and now she's here with me. She's made tea."

I hear the scrape of a mug on the counter and listen as she takes a sip. "That was a really good idea, Lilah," I tell her. I hate that I can't be there with my daughter, but at least she isn't alone. The fact that Mrs. Matthews is there with her to help her out means a lot to me. "Do you mind if I talk to her?"

"Sure." There's the sound of the phone being passed and I close my eyes, waiting.

"Dr. Bennett, how are you doing?" Mrs. Matthews's voice is warm and calming and I take another deep breath, grateful for her being with my daughter.

"I'm fine," I tell her, keeping my voice positive. "The detectives are just clearing me, that's all, but I really do appreciate you being with Lilah right now. I know that she's stressed and worried."

"She is, a little bit, but I'm more than happy to be with her. She's a very special kid, Dr. Bennett, and I'm just really glad that she called so I could come help." There's a pause and I imagine her walking across my kitchen, probably trying to put a little space between herself and Lilah while she speaks. "Do you want me to stay with her until you get home?" Her voice is a little quieter. I consider her offer.

I know that Lilah wouldn't appreciate the idea of having a babysitter, but I also know how much she likes her math teacher. It's a lot for me to ask of Mrs. Matthews, but I didn't really ask—she offered. The thought of Lilah having someone there with her when I can't be, much as I want to, calms the worry I feel brewing in the back of my mind.

"Are you sure, Mrs. Matthews?" I ask, hardly able to believe that I'm really putting this poor woman on the spot like this. She did offer, but I still hate to take her up on it.

"Please," she says with a chuckle. "Call me Carol. Really. By now I feel like I know you so well even though we've barely met." She sounds so warm and friendly that I'm suddenly overwhelmed.

I'm not normally one to cry about anything, but the thought of this kind woman going so far out of her way to take care of my daughter makes tears well up in my eyes. "Okay. Carol it is. Thank you. I'll be home around dinner time, but please, *please*. do not feel like you have to stay that long. If you and Lilah decide that she's okay—"

"I'm going to leave it up to her," she interrupts. Her voice is firm. I can only imagine how she handles her classroom and have no doubt in my mind that she rules it with an iron fist. "If she wants me to stay until you get here, then I will."

"Sounds perfect," I say, but she's already hung up. I jerk the phone from my ear and stare at the screen, fighting back the sick feeling in the pit of my stomach.

I know that she didn't cut me off on purpose. From what Lilah has said and from what I can see, she's a delightful, thoughtful, and driven woman. She's obviously filling a need that my daughter has that I'm not sure that I can meet. I'm grateful for her presence in my daughter's life.

I just wish that I was the one there with Lilah in this moment. The stress that she is under right now must be overwhelming and the thought of her worrying that the police think that I had anything to do with my former patients dying is enough to make me sick. Before Sara died I had promised her that I would do whatever it took to keep Lilah happy and safe.

I'd held her on her death bed and told her that I would make sure that our daughter was always taken care of, and for so many years, I was able to do that on my own. Sure, she's had teachers who have taken care of her during the day when she's been at school, but I've always been the one to meet her needs the rest of the time.

Both Sara and I were only children, and Lilah doesn't have any living grandparents. It's always been hard knowing that she doesn't have any family who could step in if she needed them, but up until now, she hasn't needed anyone but me.

I certainly won't be able to be her confidant about certain things as she gets older. I always knew that there would come a time when she would look to build a relationship with a woman who could better meet those needs. I'm not at all upset about that. I knew in the back of my mind that this was going to happen eventually.

I guess I'm just surprised and a little wistful that that time has finally come.

And I really wish that it were Sara at home with her, comforting her, taking care of her. I hate the thought that Lilah has to depend on someone who isn't family to protect her right now when she's feeling so vulnerable.

"Get a grip, Grey," I mutter to myself, pushing away from the wall. "Your daughter needs someone and it's not you, but that doesn't mean that you need to act like your world is ending."

Taking a deep breath, I look down at my watch. The scheduled surgery time is coming up quickly. After that, I have some post-op documentation to fill out on my computer, and then I'll be able to get home to my daughter. It tears me up inside that I'm not the one with her right now. I really hope that Mrs. Matthews will still be there when I get home.

No. Carol. She told me to call her Carol.

Hope rises in me. Maybe she can be the positive female influence that my daughter needs so badly. She treats Lilah like a granddaughter and I really should just be more grateful.

LILAH

$\mathcal{I}$ feel like a hermit for the rest of the week. I spend time with Mrs. Matthews doing algebra and cooking, but otherwise I just stay in the house. I don't really want to talk to anyone, not even my best friend. It's not that I think that anyone will think that my dad actually had anything to do with the murders, but the thought of people even wanting to talk to me about it is enough to make me sick.

It's best just to keep to myself right now. That way I won't have to answer any uncomfortable questions and I won't have to deal with anyone who might think that my dad is actually a bad guy.

Because he's not. I know that my dad loves his job and his patients and wouldn't ever do anything to hurt them. So, instead of going out and having to interact with anyone who might think something terrible about my dad, I'd much rather just stay at home.

By Saturday, I've watched every episode of the new seasons of *Meeting his Bride*, which my dad says is absolute trash and hates for me to watch but who cares, baked three batches of cookies, and read four books that I've been meaning to get to but haven't had the time to sit down and crack open.

This is not how the summer was supposed to go.

The math tutoring was bad enough because it kept me from getting to see my friends. But this is even worse. Honestly, I'd be willing to have daily math tutoring for the rest of the summer if it meant that none of these murders were taking place.

Yesterday I'd been so distracted during math that Mrs. Matthews finally called it quits and then took me out to the garden to walk me around and explain what all of the plants were. Some things surprised me, like I didn't know that you could eat nasturtium flowers. They're a little peppery and she told me to try them on a salad or a sandwich sometime. I think I might do that.

How she knows so much is beyond me. She always evades my questions about her personal life, so I really don't know very much about her. I know that she's married, that she loves teaching math, and that she's hoping to retire either before this next school year or immediately after it. That's it.

It's Saturday morning but I haven't heard my dad moving around yet, so I slip out of bed, opening up my laptop. My fingers hover above the keys for a moment as I think about searching online for her. I don't know why I want to know more about her. It's probably that she doesn't really talk about her past.

Before I can press a single key, though, there's a knock on my bedroom door, and I shut the laptop before spinning around in my chair.

"Hey, Lilah," my dad says, pushing the door open. My whole life I've never locked it or shut it completely. Even though I don't really get nightmares anymore and I certainly don't cry out for him if something is wrong, I still like knowing that he's right down the hall and there to help me if I need him. "I thought that you might be up. You getting hungry?"

I shake my head. My appetite has definitely taken a hit with everything that's been going on. "I'm good, Dad," I say, "but thanks. Feel free to make something for yourself and I'll be down in a bit."

He nods, his eyes flicking briefly up to my face before he pushes the door further shut. He's concerned, I can tell, but I don't want him to worry about me, not when he's so wrapped up in thinking about his murdered patients.

The best thing for me right now is just to keep my head down and try not to cause any trouble.

With that thought in mind, I open my laptop back up, but instead of searching for Mrs. Matthews, I click over to the local news. I know that my dad wouldn't want me following the murder investigations so closely, but I can't seem to stop myself.

I know there isn't a chance that I could ever solve them before the police do, but it still feels good to be keeping an eye on what's going on and making sure that there isn't anything that could possibly point to my dad. I take a sip of my water from the glass I always have on my desk, then turn my attention back to the computer.

Local man found dead in back yard, foul play suspected.

The water turns into a hard rock in my throat and I have to swallow hard to force it down. It burns all the way down to my stomach, where it sits like a piece of jagged rock, making me feel ill. I don't want to read any further but I maneuver the mouse to the headline anyway, taking a deep breath before I finally click on it.

"Please don't be one of my dad's patients," I whisper, my eyes skimming the article. I don't know the names of all of the people that he's operated on in his career, but I'm still hoping that I'll be able to tell from the article whether or not this has anything to do with my dad. "Oh, please, please, please..."

My voice trails off and I just stare when I get to the last line of the article. *Police believe that this may be connected to a trio of other recent murders.*

"Dad?" I call, unsure if he'll even be able to hear my voice downstairs. Nothing happens, so I clear my throat and try again. "Dad!"

"Lilah?" His voice sounds like he's at the bottom of the stairs. A moment later I hear him running up them. He's taking them two at a time, which isn't something that I've heard him do in a really long time.

Then again, I don't know that I've ever called out for him like this before, with such fear and panic in my voice. This time, instead of knocking at my door, he throws it open and crosses the room straight to me.

"Lilah, what's wrong? Are you hurt?" He grabs my shoulders and kneels down in front of me, his eyes flicking over my body, looking for blood.

"There was another murder," I whisper, even though it's almost impossible for me to speak the words.

Slowly, his eyes leave mine and drift to the news story. I watch as all of the color drains from his face. His cheeks were slightly red from running to get to me but they're pale now, his eyes dark and sunken above his cheeks. I swear, he ages ten years in these few seconds right in front of me as he tries to grasp what he's seeing on my computer.

"Please tell me he wasn't your patient," I whisper, but from the look on his face, I already know the answer.

There's no way that he'd look so sick at the news of there being another murder otherwise.

"Lilah," he begins, but he doesn't get a chance to finish. Before he can say anything more, the sound of the doorbell ringing fills the house.

GREY

"*D*r. Bennett, are you home?" The detective's voice is so loud that I can hear it through the front door. Even though I told Lilah to stay upstairs and wait for me to come back, I know that she's followed me down. She's not in the living room, but I can picture her peeking in from around the door frame.

The man in the news article was my patient. Of course he was. He didn't require a transplant, unlike the other three murder victims, but I still treated him, performed an ablation as well as put in a stent.

Taking a deep breath, I unlock the door and swing it open before Detective Laite can knock again. I have no doubt in my mind that she would love to knock and call for me as loudly as possible so that everyone in the entire neighborhood would look out their windows and see what's going on.

She's not subtle, that's for sure.

"Good morning, Detective," I say, keeping my voice calm, measured and even. "What can I do for you?"

She looks exhausted, like she was out all night, but

manages to grin at me. There's another detective standing partly hidden behind her, and he matches the description of the one Lilah said came to the house perfectly. He glances at me like he's bored, then looks past me into the house.

Shifting my weight from one foot to another, I do my best to block his view of the living room. He won't see anything that will incriminate me, but I don't want him seeing Lilah standing there, her eyes wide, watching what's going on. I'm her father, and my one job in life is to protect her. I don't want this man staring at her.

"You can come with us to the station to answer a few questions," Detective Laite says. "I'm sure that you saw the news this morning?"

I could lie to her and tell her that I have no idea what she's talking about, but she strikes me as the type of person who can easily see when someone isn't telling the truth.

Across the street I see a curtain in the neighbor's front window shift slightly to the side.

"We just did," I say. "Terrible stuff. Hopefully your team is getting closer to figuring out who's behind these killings and stopping them."

"We're about as close as we can be without getting bitten on the nose," she says, slowly breaking into a smile. "Now, Dr. Bennett, are you going to come with us quietly and sit nicely in the car or do I need to get out the hand-cuffs?" Her hand moves to the cuffs on her duty belt.

It's obvious from the look on her face that she would love nothing more than to put me in cuffs on my own front porch and lead me down to her waiting car. Even as I think that, though, I decide that she's bluffing. If she were going to arrest me, she'd arrest me.

"I'll come with you, of course," I tell her. "It will feel good to clear my name." I'm doing my best to keep as calm as possible even though my heart is slamming in my chest so hard I wouldn't be surprised if she could hear it. It's difficult for me to think straight right now, much less concentrate on how I'm going to go with her without getting physically sick. "May I talk to my daughter first?"

"You can call her here to the door," the detective says. "I'll be right here with you."

Of course she wouldn't want to let me disappear back into the house. She honestly believes that I killed four people and she'd be stupid to let me out of her sight for one moment. Luckily, I know that Lilah is right behind me.

"Lilah?" I call, turning around to look for her. "Would you come here, please?"

Dressed in her pajamas still, with her hair unbrushed and a frightened look on her face, Lilah looks younger than she has in years. For just a moment, she looks just as child-like and innocent as she did when her mom was still alive.

"Dad, this can't be happening," she says, running up to me and throwing her arms around me. Her face is bright with tears and she grips me tightly. After a moment, she pulls back, turning to glare at the detectives.

"He didn't do this, you know! I don't know why you think he did, but he didn't. He wouldn't. Besides, he was here all night long with me, so are you going to arrest me as an accessory to murder? You're letting a murderer go free by focusing on my dad. Don't you see that?"

She sounds as frantic as I feel, but I know that her acting out like that in front of the detectives will not do anything to help.

"Lilah," I say, taking her by the arms and pulling her so that she has to look at me. "You need to stay calm and listen to me, okay? I'm going to go with them and answer their questions. We both know that I didn't, wouldn't, couldn't do this. They'll see that I'm innocent and then I'll come back as soon as possible."

She gives me a little nod, sniffing hard to try to keep from crying. My poor girl, even though she's trying hard to be brave, she still has tears streaking down her cheeks. She can't stop them from leaking out but she's refusing to look weak by reaching up and wiping them away.

She's so much like Sara sometimes that it almost kills me.

"I want you to call Mrs. Matthews." The words are out of my mouth before I even realize that I'm going to say them. "Tell her what's going on and ask her to come stay at the house with you, okay?" I know that the neighbors are all watching and would love nothing more than to be invited over to spend time with Lilah so they could pump her for information, but I'm not doing that. They're vultures. Carol, however, really cares about Lilah.

"I can do that," she sniffs. "What else?"

"Nothing." I lean forward and press a kiss onto her forehead. "Tell her how much I appreciate it and that I'll make it up to her somehow, okay? She really cares for you, Lilah, you know that, right? I have no doubt in my mind that she'll do whatever she can to make sure that you're safe and taken care of."

"I love you, Dad," she says, and throws her arms around me again.

Even though I know that the detectives are probably getting impatient to go, I wrap my arms around my daughter and hug her back long and hard. She needs to be hugged and held more than they need me to leave with them right now.

"Dr. Bennett." Detective Laite's voice is a low warning, and I regretfully let Lilah go.

"Lock the doors," I tell her. "Call Mrs. Matthews, okay? Can you do that?"

She nods. "I can. I love you."

"I love you too, Lilah." I have to leave before I start to cry. I can't let her see that. I turn away abruptly and follow the silent detective to the waiting car. It's unmarked, sleek and black with heavily tinted windows, and he opens the back door for me to get in.

"I just want to see that she shuts the door, if I may," I say to him, turning and looking back up at the house. Lilah is still framed in the doorway and I wave at her. "Go inside, okay?"

She does, slamming the door hard. For a moment, I just stand there, wanting to make sure that she isn't about to come back out. When she doesn't, I turn and get into the car, hardly noticing the smooth seats or the air conditioning pumping through the vehicle. Even as we pull away, my eyes are locked on the front door, hoping to get one more look at my daughter.

CAROL

*M*ost people my age would want to sleep in on a Saturday morning to make up for the lost sleep during the week. And most people who just spent part of the night out killing someone would want to sleep in to try to be as refreshed as possible in the morning. But not me.

At least, that's what I'm assuming. It's not like there's some national association of murderers that I could join. I can only imagine the meetings and the conference topics. So much more interesting than the ones for math teachers.

Instead of *Differentiation in the Classroom*, there might be *Pros and Cons of Killing Close to Home* or even *How to Hide a Body in Plain Sight*.

So sue me, I'm a little punchy.

I already have three cups of coffee pumping through my veins and I have a very good feeling that today might be the day that I finally get what I want. I hadn't thought that it would take four victims for the police to really home in on Dr. Bennett. After they stopped by the hospital this past week to talk to him, I'd thought for sure that they were going to take him in for questioning and was disappointed when they didn't.

The murder of poor Ricky Valdez is all over the news. I couldn't find another heart transplant patient in the area, but he had a lot of work done by Dr. Bennett, so I'm pretty sure that his death will get the point across. I'm keeping the news on in the kitchen, enjoying listening to the anchors speculate about who the murderer is and who might be next, but I'm much more interested in my cell phone.

It hasn't rung yet, which is a bit frustrating. I could have stayed in bed for a while longer, just stretching and enjoying the day before it got started, but I wanted to be sure that I'd be up and ready for when Lilah called.

Do I know for sure that she's going to call? Not really. I can't even guarantee that the police will go talk to her dad this morning and then take him in for questioning, but I have a pretty good feeling that that's what's going to happen. It's frankly negligent of them to let me get away with killing this many people before stepping in to do something.

I thought that by now everything would be moving along for me.

I hate the waiting.

Frustrated, I empty the remains of my coffee into the sink, then rinse out my cup, swirling and dumping the water before putting the whole thing in there to wash later. It's not that I think that Trent will actually ever wash them for me, but if Lilah does call in a panic then I have to admit that I enjoy the thought of my husband being faced with a sink full of dirty dishes.

I'm about to try to read a book when my phone rings.

"Finally, you little brat," I mutter. Lilah took her sweet time reaching out to me and that makes me nervous. "Lilah?

Good morning!" I paste a huge smile on my face before answering the call to make sure that I sound really happy to hear her.

"Mrs. Matthews?" she gulps. She's been crying, that much is obvious right away. She sounds terrible, the poor thing, and that tells me everything that I need to know.

They came and took her dad. Finally.

"Lilah? Are you okay? What's wrong?" There's so much concern and love in my voice that I think for a moment about going into voice acting. I know that I'm a little old to be on screen for a movie, but voices of all ages are necessary. Nobody would judge me for being older if they fell in love with my voice.

"It's my dad," she says, hiccuping so hard that it's difficult to make out her words. "The detectives came by and took him in for questioning this morning."

I wait a moment, like I have to absorb the information that she just gave me, then let out a small gasp. "What? Why? Didn't they bother him enough when they talked to him earlier this week? What in the world could they possibly want with your poor father?"

Lilah's breathing deeply, like she's trying her best to control her emotions. "There was another murder, Mrs. Matthews, and they took him to the station to talk to him. He didn't do it, though! He was right here with me the entire time. He wouldn't—" She lets out a sob and I wait for her to compose herself before I speak.

"I'm coming over," I say firmly. "You just sit tight, Lilah, and I'll be right there. There's no way that you should have to face this day alone."

"Are you sure? He wanted me to call and ask you to come over, but you don't have to. I don't want to ruin your weekend."

"You are the most important thing right now," I tell her, and in my mind I can see myself accepting my Oscar. "Don't open the door for anyone, okay? I'm getting my keys right now." My keys and my purse have in fact been sitting by the front door since last night in anticipation of this phone call. As I continue speaking to her, I leave my kitchen and grab them from the small table. "I'm on my way, okay?"

"Thank you. Mrs. Matthews, really, thank you. I don't know what my dad and I would do without you. You're a total lifesaver."

"Don't mention it. Just stay in the house, Lilah." I hang up before she can answer and slip my phone into my purse. So it took a little bit longer this morning to get going. Things are looking up now.

"I'm leaving," I call out, but I keep my voice quiet. Trent loves to sleep in on weekends and probably won't move for a few more hours. By the time he gets up I should have a better idea about how much the Bennetts need me and I might be able to tell him that I won't be coming home for a while.

He'll get over it. All he really wants to do is play golf and watch TV, so it's not like he'll miss me. By calling out to him that I'm leaving, though, I can truthfully tell him later that I let him know I was going, just he must have been so out of it that he forgot.

One more look around the house, then I'm out the front door. I've driven to the Bennett house so many times recently that I make the turns without even thinking about where I'm going. In my mind I'm going over the details of last night, just to make sure that I didn't make any mistakes.

I know that I didn't, though. All of the skills that I need to handle myself and get away with murder are skills that my parents taught me when I was little. Even so, I never would have considered going down this path if it weren't for my poor George and what Dr. Bennett did to him.

I hate that he won't ever go to trial for murdering the one man I've ever loved, but seeing him behind bars and knowing that I'm the reason he's there will make me feel better about everything.

It won't bring George back, but it will give me some closure.

Lilah flings open the door as soon as I start walking up the front porch steps. She must have been looking through the window for me, although I never noticed the curtains twitch.

"Mrs. Matthews, you came!" she cries, running to me and throwing her arms around me. I hug her back, pulling her as close to me as possible.

"Of course I came, Lilah," I tell her, reaching up and lightly rubbing her back. "There's no way on earth that I would ever let you go through something like this on your own." I pause, weighing my next words. They're ones that need to be said because I know that they'll help me get what I want next, but I'm not sure if right now is the perfect time yet.

I risk it anyway. "You're like a granddaughter to me," I tell her. Her arms loosen for a moment as she looks up at me but then she squeezes me again, harder than before. "I won't let anything bad happen to you, okay? I don't know what's going on with your dad, but you're not going to have to worry about a thing. I'm here for you, Lilah, no matter what you need."

"Thank you." She's quiet for a moment, still hugging me tight. "I love you, Mrs. Matthews. I don't know what I would do without you."

There. I did time it correctly, even though I was a little bit worried about it. It was probably silly to be worried, especially when everything else has been going perfectly. "I love you, too, Lilah. I'm not leaving you until your dad is back home to take care of you, okay?"

"Thank you." Her voice is a tiny whisper and I'm glad that she can't see the satisfied grin look on my face.

Everything is working out exactly the way that I wanted it to.

LILAH

*M*rs. Matthews made us breakfast and then together we made lunch. I've showered and picked up my room, and now I feel like wandering around the house. I can't seem to quiet down because nothing feels right to do.

It's like my body isn't really mine. I feel unsettled, like there's something else I should be doing instead. When I tried reading, I couldn't concentrate on the words for more than ten minutes. Mrs. Matthews suggested we work on a puzzle, but I couldn't find one that I wanted to do.

Then we tried going for a walk, but by the end of the block I knew that everyone in the neighborhood was watching from between their window blinds. Finally she made a huge bowl of popcorn and pulled me to the sofa, telling me to put something on that would make us laugh.

The one thing that she made me promise was not to turn on the news. I wasn't planning on it, but it's nice to know that she wouldn't let me even if I tried. I like her looking out for me.

So now I've been sprawled on the sofa for two hours,

stuffing my face with popcorn, mindlessly watching something on Comedy Central. The only thing is that there's nothing that can actually make me laugh right now. I can't seem to relax enough to enjoy the show and I honestly feel like I'm going to be sick.

"Lilah," Mrs. Matthews finally says, turning off the TV and turning to look at me. "What can I do for you? This is terrible, I know, but we'll hear from your dad as soon as he can call. In the meantime, tell me, please, how can I help?"

I twist my fingers together and look up into her kind face. I know that she cares, but it's still really hard for me to open up to her. Part of me feels guilty, like I'm not honoring my mom's memory by doing that, but then I remember what my mom said to me one day. I think it might be one of my earliest memories of her.

It was in Pre-K and I'd gotten hurt on the playground. I remember falling from the slide and not being able to catch myself. When I hit the ground I just lay there for the longest time, doing my best to try to catch my breath. It hurt so bad that when I finally was able to breathe, I couldn't stop crying.

Then Miss Winters, my very young, very fresh-faced teacher, ran up to me and scooped me up from the ground, holding me close to her chest. "Lilah," she said, carrying me to a bench so that she could hold me. "Talk to me. What happened? Are you okay?"

I fought her. Shame fills me now as I think about it. She was just being kind and loving but my body ached and I wanted nothing more than to have my mom there right at that moment.

"Did someone hurt you?" She'd asked, staring at me. I wasn't sure if she had a feeling what had really happened or was just guessing. For my part, I wasn't about to tell her that

Tara Rhodes had pushed me from the slide. The only person I wanted to talk to was my mom. So I didn't answer.

When Mom picked me up from school and I told her in the car on the way home what happened, she'd pulled over on the side of the road and gotten in the back of the car with me.

I still remember how soft her touch was when she pushed my hair back from my forehead. "Lilah," she'd said, her voice full of love, "I won't always be around for you to talk to. Talking to someone else doesn't mean that you don't love me, and it certainly doesn't mean that I'm not there for you. As you get older you will have more and more people around you who want to help you. Let them in, darling."

So that's what I am remembering now, as I try to tell myself that opening up to Mrs. Matthews and talking to her about what's going on isn't hurtful or disrespectful to my mom's memory.

I turn so suddenly to face Mrs. Matthews that I'm sure she's as surprised as I am. "I don't know exactly what you can do," I tell her, squeezing the fingers of my right hand with my left. It hurts a little bit but the pain actually feels good, like it's grounding me. "But I do know that my dad wouldn't kill anyone. I told the detectives that this morning, but they didn't believe me. They still took him."

As terrifying as this is, the stuff of nightmares, it's real life. There's no pinching myself to wake up from it, no hiding from the terror that our family is going to face. I'll just have to be strong.

"It's not fair," Mrs. Matthews agrees, gently taking my hands in her own. Her skin is so warm and I actually feel myself relax at her touch. She pats the back of my hand as she talks, looking me right in the eyes. "It's terrible, Lilah, but I have no reason to believe that they will keep your dad for long. He's innocent. We both know that. We just have to wait for them to see it too."

I nod, exhaling hard. She's right. Of course she's right. She's exactly the person that I need here with me right now if I can't have my mom or my dad. "How much longer do you think that we'll have to wait? I'm sure that your husband wants you back home and I feel terrible keeping you from him."

She gives me a soft smile and shakes her head. "Don't you worry one bit about him, Lilah. Men sometimes like to pretend that they're helpless without us, but they can fend for themselves better than you'd think. I'll be here as long as you need me, okay?"

I nod. "They won't keep Dad overnight, will they?" It's a terrible thought and one that I don't want to even give voice to, but I have to. If they keep him overnight then I don't know what I'll do. I know for a fact that I won't be able to sleep and I'll just be terrified the entire time.

At the same time, though, I also know that I can't possibly ask Mrs. Matthews to stay over. She's already doing more than she has to, and asking her to stay the night is really too much.

It's like she can read my mind. "If they keep him overnight, which I'm sure they won't, then I'll stay with you," Mrs. Matthews says with a firm nod. When I open my mouth to protest, she stops me. "No arguing, Lilah. There's no way that I'd ever let you be alone at a time like this. Okay?"

It's silly but I can't help how relieved I feel. I nod and then lean forward, hoping that she'll pull me in for a hug. I just need to feel safe right now. To my relief, Mrs. Matthews grabs me and pulls me to her, wrapping her arms tightly around me. For the first time since they took Dad, I feel myself really relax.

"I'll keep you safe no matter what," she tells me. Her voice is so kind and caring that I have no reason not to believe her.

GREY

The room that I've been in all day reminds me of a
jail cell, even though Detective Laite insisted
that I'm not under arrest. She reminded me over and over
again that I came here of my own volition, and although
technically she's right, it really didn't feel that way when
she and Detective Tanner showed up at my house this
morning.

The wooden chair that I'm sitting on is hard, like a
church pew. I've shifted position so many times that my
muscles are sore from trying to keep my legs from falling
asleep, but it can't be much longer, can it? Detective Laite
told me to sit tight—like I have a choice—and that she'd be
right back.

I'm tired and I just want to get home. Even though I
know that I can leave at any time because she made that
perfectly clear, there's a voice in the back of my head telling
me that I need to wait this out. I don't know if leaving right
now would make me look guilty, but I'm not really keen on
finding out.

The fact that she showed up at my house so early this

morning and asked me to come to the station to talk scares me. From all of the true crime documentaries I've watched with Lilah, I know that detectives only really do that when they think that they have a bead on someone. There's no reason for her to ask me to come down here otherwise.

Just thinking about Lilah makes me feel ill. I have no doubt that she's safe, since Mrs. Matthews is with her right now, but that doesn't change the fact that I should be the one at home with her. I hate the thought that all this is going on and I'm not even there to comfort her.

The sound of the door swinging open makes me look up and Detective Laite walks in, disappointment written all over her face.

"You're free to go, Doctor," she says. It's obvious that she doesn't relish the idea of watching me walk out of the station door. "But I want you to know that I'm going to be keeping an eye on you. Anything that you do that looks suspicious, I'll see it. I'll know if you pick your nose in the dark and what you eat for a midnight snack, do you understand?"

"I do." Planting my hands on the table, I slowly push myself up. My body aches and I'm pretty sure that the pounding in my head will only be cleared by a solid ten hours of sleep, but at least I'm getting out of here. "But I promise you, Detective Laite, I have nothing to hide. You're going to get really bored watching me all the time."

"I doubt that." She steps out of the door so that I can walk past her but doesn't move enough that I can slip by her without my elbow bumping into hers. I have no doubt that it was intentional but I don't respond. Not worth it.

"Detective Tanner said that he'll take first shift tonight, so he's going to drop you off at home," she says, her voice following me down the hall.

I merely raise my hand in acknowledgement and keep on walking. She can call after me all she wants, try to make me feel like I've done something wrong, but I know the truth. I don't know why she's so focused on me as the only suspect, but I know in my heart that I didn't kill anyone.

Unfortunately, that means that the killer is still out there, and may even be plotting who they're going to go after next. That thought sends a chill down my spine and is the only thing that I can think of on the ride to my house with Detective Tanner. He's silent the entire way, obviously exhausted and more than ready for bed, but that's not my problem.

I honestly don't care how tired he is. He can sit out here in his car and fall asleep for all that I care.

It's dark when I get home and I open the front door slowly, wanting to be careful not to startle Lilah if she's still up. I know that she likes to stay up a bit later on the weekend, so I wouldn't be surprised to see her reading on the sofa, but the house is already mostly dark. There's a soft glow in the kitchen that I recognize immediately as the light above the sink that we like to leave on so that we don't bump into anything if either of us wants a midnight snack.

As quietly as possible, I make my way upstairs, avoiding the one squeaky one in the middle. I keep promising Lilah that I'm going to repair it but I just haven't gotten around to it yet. Maybe it's time to call in a professional and let them take care of it for me.

Mrs. Matthews's car is still in our driveway, so I'm sure that she's in here somewhere. I glance at my bedroom, wanting nothing more than to hit the hay, but instead walk down the hall to Lilah's. Her door is slightly cracked and I push it open.

Immediately, she stirs awake.

"Dad?" She asks, a touch of fear mingled with the sleepiness in her voice. "Is that you?"

"It's me." Moving slowly because I'm so tired, I sit on the edge of her bed. "How are you, sweetpea? You hanging in there?"

She sits up to lean against me, smelling like sleep and soap. "I've been worrying all day, but Mrs. Matthews finally told me that I should go to bed and let my body rest. I didn't want to, but as soon as my head hit the pillow, I was out. How are you?"

I loop my arm around her shoulder and pull her closer to me. "I'm fine," I tell her. There's no way that I want to tell her that I now have detectives watching my every move.

She'll find that out soon enough in the morning. There's no reason to tell her now and make her worry so much that she can't get back to sleep.

"I'm just glad to be home," I say instead. "Did Mrs. Matthews come right over? Did she take care of you?"

Lilah nods. "Yeah, she was great. Wouldn't leave tonight until she knew for sure that you were coming home and I'd be okay, so I put her up in the guest room. I hope that's okay."

"It was a great idea," I tell her. "Now, you get some sleep, okay? It's midnight already. Don't feel like you have to get up early in the morning. Sleep in. Okay?"

"I love you, Dad," she says, flopping back on her bed. "I'm so glad that you're home."

"I love you too, Lilah." Carefully, I tuck the covers up around her and snuggle her into bed, just like I've done since she was a little girl. When I leave her room I leave her door ajar just a bit in case she calls for me in the night.

Walking down the hall to my room, I pass the guest room. I can hear the fan blowing. The door is shut and there isn't a light on under it, so I continue on to my room and my bed.

I'll talk to Mrs. Matthews in the morning and thank her for everything that she's done for my daughter. I have no idea how I'm going to repay her for her kindness: I have no idea if she'll even accept money if I try to give it to her, but I have to thank her for looking out for our family somehow.

As I climb into bed, I try to think of what I would have done if we hadn't had her in our lives. Lilah would have had to have called a neighbor, which I would have hated, or one of her friends, which she would have hated. Without Mrs. Matthews, there really wouldn't have been a good way to handle today.

Rolling over on my pillow, I exhale hard, then feel myself sinking into sleep.

CAROL

I'm enjoying a cup of coffee at the kitchen counter when Dr. Bennett wanders in. I almost choke on my coffee when I see him: he's got on jeans and a hoodie and he looks more like a wayward teenager than a celebrated cardiologist.

I knew that he'd come home. I noticed that his bedroom door was closed this morning when I got up and came downstairs to make some breakfast for myself. Still, it's surprising to see him standing here, looking for all the world like he just woke up after a nice restful sleep.

"You're home!" I say, setting my coffee down and hoping that he can't see the way my hand shakes. "I'm so glad. Does Lilah know?"

He nods, pouring himself a cup of coffee, then takes a seat on the stool next to me. "I checked on her last night when I got in and she woke up enough to say hi and see that I was here." He blows on his coffee then takes a sip, sighing with contentment as the taste spreads across his tongue. "It's nice to have another early bird in the house for once."

"Oh, I'm not good at sleeping," I tell him. "Too many things to do. But now that you're home, I'll get out of your hair. I hope that it's okay that I stayed over, I simply didn't want to leave Lilah alone, especially not at night."

"No, you did exactly the right thing."

When I make a move to leave, he turns his head to me. "Wait, Carol, let me talk to you for a moment if you don't mind. I can't thank you enough for what you did yesterday. I know that you're Lilah's teacher and you've been tutoring her this summer and all, but you really went above and beyond."

"It was nothing," I say, but I don't move. I want to hear how the great Dr. Bennett is going to thank me for taking such good care of his only child. "It was what anyone would have done in the situation."

Although I don't really know about that. Our situation is definitely not one that I think a lot of people have come across before. It's, shall we say, unique.

"That's not true," he says. "Not everyone would have done that. Lilah really looks up to you, Carol. She loves spending time with you. You make her feel special and that's important, especially at her age. How in the world can I ever thank you for what you've done for her?"

"Your checks are more than enough," I tell him. "More than I ever expected, really. I wanted to help Lilah with her math to make sure that she's prepared enough to do well in the fall, and I never thought that you'd be so generous with the payment. Really, it's almost too much."

"This is more than tutoring, though," he says, getting up and walking over to the refrigerator. "You've been taking care of my daughter when I simply couldn't. I don't know how to put a price on that but I'm willing to pay you whatever you want for your time."

Well, he said it, not me. I was taking care of Lilah when he couldn't. I did what he couldn't—stepped up and made sure that his daughter was okay. Even though it feels really good to hear him say it, I don't expect him to really follow through on paying me for this weekend. So I simply flash him my best smile.

"Please, Dr. Bennett, don't worry yourself one moment about it. Lilah is a really special girl and getting to spend time with her is just as much of a blessing to me as a help to her. I love talking to her and getting to know her better." I pause, doing my best to look the slightest bit worried about what I'm going to say next. "In fact, being with Lilah this weekend was really good for me, too."

My voice cracks there at the end and I see the look of concern flash on Dr. Bennett's face. "Carol, what's going on? Are you okay? If you have a problem that you need help with, I hope that you know that you can ask me for anything and I'll help you however I can."

Perfect. "No, I'm fine," I say, flapping my hand dismissively at him. "Don't you worry about a silly old lady." Picking up my coffee cup, I walk it across the kitchen to put it in the sink, but he takes it from me and tops it up, putting his hand on my upper back to guide me back to the counter.

"No, something's wrong. You've cared for Lilah so much recently, I feel like you're part of the family now. One thing that you need to know about the Bennetts, we never leave family behind. It's just not how we operate. Talk to me."

I sit and sniff, adjusting my hold on my coffee cup a few times before looking up at him. "Well, if you really don't think that I'm going to be a burden..."

"You are not a burden." He leans on the counter, resting his elbows on it while he looks at me. "Talk to me. Let's figure out how we can get you some help. I'm not going to leave you hanging right now, Carol. It's not how the Bennetts do things."

"Thank you." I take a shuddering breath. "You know that I'm married?" I ask, pointing at the ring on my finger. Dr. Bennett nods and I continue. "I thought that Trent was the one for me. He's always been kind to me, but the past few years, that's changed. I told him that I'd be here helping Lilah and he got violent, told me that I shouldn't bother coming home. I haven't been answering his phone calls, but I did listen to his voicemails. He found the papers I had hidden in my bedside table."

"What kind of papers?" Dr. Bennett looks so concerned for me that I have to fight down the grin threatening to appear on my face. Another Oscar acceptance speech plays through my head.

"Divorce papers," I manage. "I signed them with the lawyer a few months ago but I haven't been brave enough to give them to him and ask him for a divorce. But now he knows, of course, and...he's mad."

"Oh, Carol." He pats my hand and I look up at him, trying to give him a weak smile. "I had no idea. This whole time I've been so wrapped up with work and then with the detectives that it honestly never crossed my mind that you would have something so terrible going on in your own life."

"I'll be fine," I say, giving him a brave smile. "Really, Dr. Bennett, I'm going to be fine."

"Call me Grey. Have you talked to the police about this? Do they know what's going on?"

I shake my head emphatically. If the police got involved then they'll hear the real story, which is that I left the divorce papers on the counter yesterday when I came over to be with Lilah. Trent's boring, like wet toast, and he's never raised his voice or his hand at me, but I know that I need to leave him behind me if I'm going to have the best chance at the rest of my plan working.

"I don't think that I can call the police," I tell him. "You know that you can't always...trust them to do the right thing."

Dr. Bennett's face falls and I know that I've hit a nerve with what I just said. That's exactly what he's dealing with right now. I can practically see the gears working in his mind as he thinks about what I just said.

"Well, you're just going to have to move in with us," he tells me, with a nod. "We have plenty of space, Lilah loves having you around, and you need to get out of your house. Simple."

"Dr. Bennett—"

"Grey." He cuts me off and pins me in place with his stare.

"Okay, Grey, that's incredibly kind of you, but it's just not something that I can do. I don't want to step on toes or get in the way here. You and Lilah are a family and there's no way that I can move in without upsetting that balance. It's okay, I'll be fine. I'll stay somewhere else or get a hotel or something."

"Not a chance." His voice is firm and smacks the counter once with his open palm like that's going to put an end to my arguing. "Do you know when he'll be away from the house today? We'll get over there and move whatever you need to feel comfortable here."

"He'll be gone all day," I say slowly, "according to the messages that he left me. Apparently, he was going to go visit his sister for a day or so."

The truth is that Trent will be on the golf course all day. He's probably been there for an hour already, and I imagine that he won't be home until late tonight. He'll be heartbroken when he sees the divorce papers, of course, but I can't worry about that. Trent isn't a terrible man, but he isn't George.

And all of this is for George.

LILAH

By the time Sunday dinner rolled around, everything in our house had completely changed. Mrs. Matthews moved into the guest room down the hall, bringing with her a few suitcases packed haphazardly with her clothes and toiletries. I wanted to sit in her room and talk to her while she unpacked, but my dad had pulled me into the living room to talk to me.

"She's going through a really tough time," he'd told me, keeping his voice low so that she couldn't possibly hear what we were saying. "And we need to respect that and give her the space that she needs to deal with whatever she's feeling right now, okay? I know that it's hard, Lilah, but let her breathe."

Let her breathe. That's what my dad always used to say to my mom when I would fall or get hurt. She wanted to pull me to her chest and try to make me feel better and he'd pull her back a little bit, keeping her from smothering me.

"Let her breathe, Sara," he'd say, even though both my mom and I would be in tears at that point. I'd be crying because it hurt and she'd be crying because she wanted to hold me.

I never told her that he was right, that letting me breathe and making sure that I had room to catch my breath really helped me. There wasn't any way that I could look my mom in the eyes and make her think that I didn't want her right there with me all the time.

Dad knew, though. He always did.

One time that really sticks out to me is when I was five and had climbed up into the huge oak tree in the backyard. My mom was really sick by then and we were all dealing with it in our own ways. For my mom, that meant trying to keep up her normal routine even though her body revolted against it. For my dad, that meant spending as much time trying to help her as he could.

Me? I just wanted away from it all. I wanted to get away from the sickly hospital smell that was all over her when she came home, and the way that her arms and legs were so thin I could practically reach my hands around them. Hiding in a tree seemed like the best idea at the time and I remember pushing myself to climb as high as possible.

Even as the ground stretched away far below me and I knew that I'd gone too far, I stubbornly pushed myself to pull up on the next branch. The rough bark cut into the soft skin on my hands but I honestly didn't care at the time. If anything, it felt good. It made me feel like I was still alive and like I could face whatever was coming my way.

"Lilah!" My mom's voice was so weak now when she yelled that I could have easily pretended that I didn't hear her and just kept my face towards the bright blue sky and keep pulling myself up the tree.

But I looked down at her.

I hadn't realized just how high up I really was. I knew

that I was higher than I'd ever been before, but the effect of looking away from the sky and down past my feet, which were snuggled tightly up against the trunk of the tree, made me feel sick and dizzy all of a sudden.

Without meaning to, I let go. I remember looking at my hands in surprise and trying to will my fingers to grab back onto the tree but I couldn't seem to do it. I watched as my hands pulled away from the trunk and then I felt nothing but weightlessness.

Now that I'm older, I know that I really didn't fall as far as I think that I did. It felt like I was really high up in the tree, and for a little kid I guess I was, but in truth I probably only fell about ten feet. It was still enough for me to land on my arm and hear the sickening crack when it snapped under me.

Immediately, my mom threw herself at me, but she was too weak to pull me to her. I wanted to be in her arms, wanted her to somehow make the pain stop, but she couldn't lift me from the ground and I couldn't seem to push myself up from the earth to turn into her embrace.

So she lay down on top of me. My mom stretched her body out on mine, doing her best to comfort me and hold me even though she couldn't pick me up. Our combined screaming brought my dad running out of the house. He pulled my mom from me, telling her to give me room to breathe, then picked me up like a rag doll.

I hardly remember the trip to the hospital or what happened there. We have plenty of pictures of my arm in a bright pink cast, scribbled on by my friends who wanted to sign it, but I don't remember much about that time.

What I do remember was the crushing feeling of my mom pressing me to the ground and the way that my dad had screamed for her to give me room to breathe. Her stretched out on me, trying her best to save me, was almost as scary as the fact that I had a shooting pain my arm that was worse than anything I'd ever known.

I don't want to make Mrs. Matthews feel that same helpless feeling that I had felt. I want to be with her and see what I can do to help her out, but I don't want to smother her. I have to give her room to breathe.

So instead I help my dad put together dinner. It would be easy to assume that Mrs. Matthews would want to help because she loves to be busy in the kitchen, and I voice that to my dad. "You know," I say, stirring the flavor packet into a cup of mayo to mix into the pasta salad I'm making, "Mrs. Matthews loves to cook. Don't you think that she'd want to help out?"

My dad is chopping veggies to sauté and he stops, clutching the knife in his hand while looking at me. "I think that Mrs. Matthews is going through a huge life change right now," he says, obviously choosing his words as carefully as possible. "We can support her by not asking her to do too much, okay?"

I nod, my face red. "Right. Sorry. I just thought she'd want to help, that's all."

My dad stops and puts the knife down, reaching for me to turn me to him. "Your teacher is going through a lot," he says, his voice so low that I have to lean forward to hear what he's saying. "Not only is she dealing with major trauma at home, but she's also stepping in here to help us, and that's exhausting."

"Help us?" I frown at him. "She helped yesterday, but it's over now, isn't it? I thought that the detectives had moved on from bothering you because they don't have any evidence against you."

My heart beats wildly in my chest as I look at my dad

and wait for him to respond. It's obvious that there's something big on his mind and I want to push him to make him talk, but I know that he won't until he's completely ready.

"Lilah," he says slowly, "I'm sure that you've noticed the car parked out front?"

"That's them?" I saw the black car sitting out there, but honestly haven't paid it any mind. The neighbors always have people coming and going from their houses and it never crossed my mind that the car could be anything other than a visitor.

My dad nods, his face tight and drawn. He's never looked old, but once again it strikes me that he's aged about ten years in the past few weeks. There are lines around his eyes and on his forehead that weren't there before. I don't know how quickly a person's hair can go white, but I can't help but think that the hair on his temples looks a little bit grayer than it did before.

"They told me that they were going to be watching me," he says. "Even though I haven't done anything wrong and they don't have any proof of me hurting anyone, they made it clear that they were going to stick around and keep an eye on me."

Suddenly, I don't want anything to eat. I know that it's not right to just leave the kitchen when my dad needs my help and I'm sure that it's rude to not come to dinner, but I can't handle even looking at food right now. "I have to go," I say, stumbling out of the room.

"Lilah," he starts, but I shake my head and he sighs, running a hand through his hair. "Fine. I know that this is hard, okay? Just...please don't leave the house. I can't handle the thought of anything happening to you."

"But it wouldn't, would it?" I snap. "We have guards that moved in to the neighborhood, apparently, so I'm sure nothing bad could happen." I don't know why I'm lashing out at my dad. He certainly doesn't deserve it, but I can't help it. Spinning away from him, I race out of the kitchen, charge up the stairs, run to my room, and then launch myself onto my bed with a big bellyflop.

My stomach rumbles and I know that I'm going to be hungry later, but I don't care about that and I don't care how rude I'm being. I just can't face anyone right now.

CAROL

I hear Lilah stampede down the hall past my room and count to ten before opening my door and following her. She'd slammed her bedroom door hard enough to make the art on the walls rattle and shake, but nothing fell, so I carefully tap on her door.

"Lilah?" I call gently, raising my voice enough so that I'm sure she'll be able to hear me. She's like any other girl her age, so I'm sure that she's face down on her bed, sobbing into her pillow about how awful her life is and how much her dad doesn't love her.

There's silence for a moment and then she opens the door just a crack. It's just enough for her to be able to peek out at me, but I can see her tear-stained face. She's doing everything that she can to keep from crying, gulping down huge swallows of air like that's actually going to make her feel better.

It won't. I've survived the worst grief that a person can, and I know that you can't fight it. It's normal to want to keep your head above water and try to power your way through the pain, but that never works. The only thing that helps when you're so upset about something is to let the grief pull you down and engulf you. You have to let it fill you, run through you.

It's hard, but it's the only way to survive it. That, and antidepressants.

Looking at Lilah, I can't help but think back to when George died. I was so young when I lost him, older than Lilah is, of course, but still in the prime of my life. When Dr. Bennett killed him I sat alone for a long time in our house with the curtains drawn, letting the shadows creep across the walls.

I didn't want to see anyone, and I certainly didn't want to talk to anyone. Once I realized that my true purpose was to stop Dr. Bennett from doing any more harm, I had to get my head on straight. I had so many steps to take before I could really come for him.

My entire life has led up to this point. Everything that I've done, from marrying Trent to switching schools so that I could work in the one that Lilah went to, was all because of what Dr. Bennett did to me. And now I'm finally getting closer to my goal. So close that some days I can almost taste it.

I'm going to make him regret ever hurting my husband. Of course, I'm not going to kill him. He'll never look me in the eyes and know that I'm the reason that his entire life fell apart. But I'll know. That'll be enough for me.

"Lilah darling, are you okay?" I ask, reaching out and lightly touching her arm. For a moment, I think that she's going to turn and run back into her room, but she doesn't. Instead, she steps out into the hall, glancing over my shoulder furtively like she's looking for her dad, then collapses against me, her arms wrapping around me.

This was not what I expected, but it's perfect. I hold her tight, pulling her closer to me so that she can draw strength from me. "Lilah," I say after a moment, "can you talk to me? Tell me what's going on."

She inhales deeply and shakes her head before pulling away. "It's just that...I thought that this was all over, but now my dad is telling me that he doesn't want me to leave the house. He said that the detectives are still following him, and I don't get why."

I look at her steadily, doing my best to hide the smile that I feel forming at the corners of my mouth. "Your dad is just doing everything that he possibly can to keep you safe," I tell her. "As for the detectives, I have no idea what their end game is or why they're not leaving your dad alone, but that's ridiculous."

"He didn't kill those people," Lilah insists, her voice shaking a little bit. "He wouldn't do that. I don't know what I need to do to get them to see that." She sounds desperate for me to believe her and I squeeze her arms before letting her go.

"There's nothing that you can do," I tell her as gently as possible. "They'll realize that they suspect the wrong person eventually. All it will take is them watching your dad night and day while someone else dies and then your dad will be cleared."

She nods. "But what if they don't?"

"Don't what?" I know what she's getting at, but I want to hear her say it.

"Kill again? What if now they're done and my dad stays the prime suspect?"

That's exactly what's going to happen. Obviously there aren't going to be any more deaths. I'm a little surprised that the detectives have up till now missed the evidence that will put her dad behind bars, but I suppose they really are more stupid than I originally thought. I'll have to figure out a way to nudge them in the right direction ever so subtly.

"I don't know, darling, but I do know that being mad in your room isn't the answer. Listen, I'm going to move in with you two for a while until things settle down with my husband. I'm here for you, okay? Why don't the two of us go for a walk or something. How does that sound?"

She shakes her head. "Dad told me that I wasn't allowed to leave the house."

"Sure, by yourself, but what about with an adult? I'm sure he'll be fine with that. I bet that a nice walk would do you good and help you feel a bit better, what do you say?"

She stubs the tip of her sneaker into the floor. Never in my life would I allow a child to wear shoes in the house. It's a filthy habit and I fully intend to break her of it as quickly as possible. You can't wear your shoes in and track dirt all over everywhere. It's much better to take them off and wear house slippers.

That's just one of the things that I'm going to teach Lilah. Her father has done an acceptable job of raising her up until now, but I see no reason to let him continue. I'll take it from here and make sure that she turns into a wonderful and productive member of society.

"If you really think that he'll let me," she says with a small shrug. "I guess that getting outside does sound a bit nicer than being locked up in here."

"Perfect." I loop my arm through hers and coax her out of her bedroom. "Let's go downstairs and I'll explain to your dad that I think getting out in the fresh air is the best thing for you right now, okay? Who knows, he may even want to come with us."

"I doubt it," she grumbles, falling into step next to me.

"When he gets upset about something he mostly likes to be left alone. Besides, he won't want the detective to see him. He's hiding out in here. Like that's going to stop the detective from staying out there in his car."

"It's rough," I agree. At the bottom of the stairs I pull my arm from hers. "Stay here," I tell her, then walk into the living room.

Dr. Bennett is sitting on the sofa looking at a book. From the blank expression on his face it's clear that he's not really reading it, and when I walk up to him, he puts the book down and looks up at me wearily.

"Carol, can I help you?" His eyes flick from me to Lilah in the background and I'm sure that he's wondering what the two of us are up to. "Is something wrong?"

"Nothing's wrong," I assure him, giving him a big smile, "but I was going to go for a walk to stretch my legs and get some fresh air and I invited Lilah to come with me. She's a little worried that you won't want her to leave the house right now."

He lets out a sigh and runs his hand through his hair, a habit that I'm noticing he has when he's feeling a little stressed out about something. Seeing as he's going to be picked up by the police and charged with murder soon, yes, I'd say that he has more than enough to reason to be stressed.

"If you really think so, Carol, then I'm sure that it's fine. But I want her with you the entire time, okay? No running off, Lilah." He directs this last at his daughter.

Good. Grey doesn't have the strength to parent appropriately, especially not right now. Lilah seeing that her dad bends to what I want is perfect. It will show her that I'm the person she should be listening to.

"Hear that, Lilah?" I ask, turning to look at her. "I told you that we're doing the right thing. Let's go."

I don't bother giving Grey another look as I leave the house with his daughter in tow. He's not a good parent, and the faster Lilah realizes that, the easier it'll be for her when I take over.

GREY

The week moves by slowly, like someone has changed the sands of time into thick, sluggish mud. Surgeries that take three hours feel like they drag on for three days. I struggle to focus on what I'm doing, but my mind keeps drifting back to my time in the interview room with Detective Laite this weekend.

I'm innocent. I know that. I just wish I could keep a better handle on things. I can't seem to focus these days and when it's finally time for me to wash up after my last ablation of the day, it isn't until the anesthesiologist calls my name that I snap out of my thoughts and leave the operating room.

I have to get my head on straight. There's nothing wrong at home. Carol moving in is probably the best thing to happen right now. She's been keeping Lilah busy during the day, not only with school and cooking, but also with hikes in the woods around town.

I'm happy that my daughter isn't sitting at home just staring at the TV all summer long. I know that she wants to hurry up and take her algebra test so that she can have some time at the pool with her friends before the summer ends, but I'm not exactly keen on the idea. I want to keep her as close to me as possible. The thought of something happening to her at the pool terrifies me. It's an irrational fear, but there it is.

Warm water washes over my hands and I look up at the mirror in front of me. For a brief, horrifying moment, I don't even recognize the man staring back at me. He looks much older, with more gray in his hair than I've seen before. I didn't realize how rough I look.

I splash water on my face, then do it again. Suddenly I feel like I need to get cool, like I'm burning up inside my scrubs. The showers are right behind me and I'm the only one in here, so I strip down, stepping under the spray of the hot water and immediately turning it cooler.

My racing mind slows a little as the cool water flows over my skin. I didn't kill those men, but I can't get their faces out of my mind. Every night when I go to bed I see them, all of them, their faces the only things that I can focus on.

For the longest time after Sara died, I couldn't stop seeing her in my dreams. Every night when I closed my eyes, she was there, always checking in on Lilah, always making sure that I was okay. It was comforting, in a way.

This is different. These men aren't making sure that I'm okay. They're judging me, laughing at me. I feel like they want me to suffer for what happened to them even though I didn't have anything to do with it.

I turn the water even colder and grab the bar of soap, running it roughly over my skin. I've lost weight over the last three weeks, even with Carol moving in and making sure that there's a hot meal on the table every single night. I simply don't have an appetite, and even though I know that

I should eat to keep my blood sugar up, I can barely bring myself to put food in my mouth.

To an outside observer, I'm sure that I look guilty, but I can't seem to make myself eat properly or get more sleep. I'm running myself ragged but there isn't anything that I can do about it.

A knock on the bathroom door pulls me from my thoughts and I turn off the water, grabbing my towel and wrapping it around me. My skin is still wet but I don't want to take the time to towel off if there's an emergency. It's very rare that problems arise after surgery, but sometimes they do, and I have to be there for my patient if they need me.

"I'm coming," I call, stepping across the cold tile floor to the door. Normally I'd never go barefoot in a public bathroom because that's a great way to pick up a fungal infection, but right now my only concern is to get to that door as quickly as possible. If a patient is in trouble, I refuse to let them suffer longer just because I was so concerned about putting on my shoes.

"Is everything okay?" I ask, swinging the door open. I fully expect to see a nurse standing there, ready to pull me back into the OR.

But it's not a nurse on the other side of the door, or even the white coat of a doctor. All I see is a button-up shirt tucked into pants, all of it held in place by a massive belt.

Slowly, I raise my eyes to look at Detective Laite. She's grinning like a cat who just figured out how to open the bird cage, her eyes practically glistening with excitement.

"Detective Laite," I say, adjusting my grip on the towel around my waist so that I don't accidentally drop it. "What a surprise. How can I help you?"

"Doctor Grey Bennet, you're under arrest for the murders of Victor Ross, Michael Teal, Bert Pierce, and

Ricky Valdez. Anything that you do or say can and will be used against you in the court of law. I need you to come with me quietly, unless you would prefer to do this the hard way."

I swear, my vision blurs for a moment. I feel the edges of it go fuzzy and I have to hang onto the bathroom door as hard as I can to keep from falling over. Behind her are two uniformed officers, both of them looking at me like I'm the worst person they've ever met.

"It's a mistake," I finally manage to say. My tongue feels stuck to the roof of my mouth but I somehow peel it off and force the words out. "I don't know what you're trying to do, but I didn't kill those men. I wouldn't."

"What I'm trying to do is bring a murderer to justice," she tells me, leaning forward a little bit like her words are for me and for me alone. "Don't make this hard on yourself, Doctor. I highly doubt that you want to cause a scene right now, although I wouldn't mind. In fact, I'd be thrilled."

Her lips are pulled back from her teeth a little bit, making her look even more like a cat who has finally cornered its prey. It's obvious that she's drawing a lot of satisfaction from this, but I refuse to give her any more.

"Let me put on some clothes," I tell her, and she steps to the side as a male officer slips past her. I stop and stare at him. "I'm just putting on some clothes..." I begin, gesturing behind me.

"We can't let you do that without making sure that you're not going to do something that we'll all regret." Detective Laite actually has the gall to throw me a wink over the male officer's shoulder. "Make it snappy, Doctor Bennett, you and I have a lot to talk about."

I know that I can't argue with her and I certainly can't fight her. Even though I want to scream and run past them to get to Lilah, I just nod my head and turn silently into the bathroom. My mind is racing as I try to think through what I'm going to do next.

I have to call Lilah. Thank goodness Carol is there with her and can make sure that she's safe while we figure this all out.

I also need to call a lawyer, and I know just who to reach out to.

JEREMY

When the low point of your day is that the sandwich place down the street didn't put quite as many peppers on your sandwich as you wanted, then you finally know that you've made it. It took a little bit longer than I wanted it to, since I spent a fair amount of time giving back by working as a public defender, but I finally got there.

Anyone who knew me in or out of the courtroom knew that I wasn't going to spend the rest of my life defending clients who listed the back of the car as their permanent address. I've wanted something more from life from the moment I got my diploma, and I finally have it.

Stretching my back, I grin up at the sign on the office building from across the street. The new one was installed while I was out eating the only lunch that I've not had at my desk in years, so this is my first chance to see it hanging there in all its glory.

It looks great. Professional. My name on the end of it is exactly what I've wanted since day one.

Stanfield, Myers, and Alexander.

I'm about to walk across the street to see how my new office looks when my phone buzzes in my pocket. I pull it out and answer it without giving the phone number much thought. How many times have I been called from the jail since graduating law school? I know the number by heart and answer it quickly, wanting to get through the call before I get in the building.

"This is Jeremy Alexander," I say, stepping down off the curb.

"Jeremy, thank God. It's Grey Bennett."

I pull my phone from my ear to squint at it and confirm the phone number. There's no way that Dr. Bennett should be calling me from jail, but he is.

"Grey. What are you doing at the jail? Are you okay?" There's a break in the traffic and I cross the street quickly, pressing the phone hard to my ear to make sure that I can hear him over the wind.

Grey sighs and I feel my stomach drop. How many times have I heard people make that exact same sigh when they know that they're in a bad spot in life? If Grey's so worried that all he can do is sigh instead of answering me then I know that things are bad. I've seen him at his worst and I've never heard him make a sound like that.

"I need a lawyer. You know the murders recently? They were all my former patients and the police have charged me with them." He sounds stressed, which any man in his position would be. There's a note of panic to his words, like just saying them out loud is incredibly painful for him.

Swearing, I stop on the other sidewalk. A woman pushing a baby stroller walks past me and I wait until she's out of earshot before I continue. "You haven't talked to the police, have you?" It's always the first thing that I ask people when I speak to them. Even though the TV is loaded with

174

police procedural shows and true crime documentaries, I'm always amazed at how many people don't know better than to talk to the police.

"Of course not," he says, and I let out a sigh of relief. "They told me that I could make one phone call, so I called you." He pauses, and I know that there's more. "I need you to come down here, Jeremy. And I need you to call Lilah and tell her what's going on." He rattles off her number and I scribble it on a pad of paper I keep in my pocket.

I'd forgotten that he has a daughter and my heart sinks even more. It's bad enough to get arrested, but telling the family is the worst part. Women especially tend to get emotional.

"I'll take care of it. Don't you breathe a word to the cops, okay? I don't care what they promise you. Don't even tell them if you have to go to the bathroom. Also, don't accept anything from them. No water, no coffee, no snacks. They'll be looking for fingerprints and DNA."

"Okay. You're coming now?" His voice is a mix of desperate and hopeful. I want to assure him that nothing bad is going to happen to him, but I can't make that promise right now. All I can do is go to him.

"I'm on my way." Hanging up, I throw one glance up at where my shiny new office is on the second floor of the building. As much as I'd like to check it out now, there's no way that I can leave Grey hanging, not when he needs me this badly.

In the car I dial the number he gave me for Lilah. She picks up right away, caution in her voice.

"Hello?"

"Lilah, this is your dad's friend, Jeremy Alexander." There's no easy way to sugarcoat this, so I just forge ahead with what I need to tell her. "I'm heading to the jail right now to meet with your dad. He was arrested at the hospital this afternoon and called me to come and represent him. I'm a lawyer."

Silence. She doesn't answer, doesn't even breathe.

"Lilah? Are you there? Did you hear what I just said?"

"I'm here. Are you sure? I mean, are you sure that it was my dad and not somebody else? There's no reason that he'd be arrested. He didn't kill those men." There's the soft murmur of another female voice behind her and I hear the phone being handed over.

"Hello? This is Mrs. Carol Matthews. How can I help you?"

Carol Matthews. I don't know that name, but it doesn't matter. Whoever she is, she's obviously older than Lilah and sounds much more self-assured.

"Hi, Mrs. Matthews, I'm Jeremy Alexander," I say, then repeat what I just told Lilah.

"What can I do?" she asks immediately.

Thank goodness she's going to take control and isn't just going to sit there and cry. There are few things worse than trying to deal with an upset family member over the phone when I really need to just hang up and drive. "Could you possibly stay with Lilah for a bit? I'm going to go talk to Grey now and see how quickly we can clear this all up."

She chuckles. "I've actually moved in to help with just that," she says. "Don't you worry about Lilah. Tell Grey that I have everything under control here at home and that I'll take care of her. Just let me know if there's anything else that I can do, okay?"

"Text me your phone number," I say, taking the final turn into the jail's parking lot. "I'll see if Grey is okay with me talking to you and, if he is, I'll call you later."

"I'll do that right now," she says. "Thank you for taking

care of Grey. I'll handle Lilah. Please, Mr. Alexander, let us know as quickly as you can what's going on. This is simply terrible."

I hang up, park the car, and look up at the jail in front of me. It's one thing to defend someone that I've never met. In fact, I've done it so many times that I couldn't even guess how many times I've walked through those doors.

It's something else entirely to walk through those doors to defend someone that I've known for years. Grey operated on my wife years ago. It was just a simple stent, but it was the most terrifying experience of my life. Knowing that she was in such good hands was the only thing that helped me keep it all together.

Well, he took care of my wife and me then. Now it's my turn to return the favor. I have no idea what evidence the police might have against him, but there's no doubt in my mind that Grey Bennett is not a murderer.

LILAH

"What did he say?" Tears stream down my cheeks as I grab my phone back from Mrs. Matthews. Part of me appreciates that she handled things for me, but part of me hates that I don't have a clue what's going on right now. "Is my dad really under arrest? How can they do this to him?"

My voice is getting higher and higher the more that I speak but I don't care. Turning my phone over in my hand, I stare at the screen accusingly like it's the phone's fault that this is happening.

"He's going to go meet with your dad right now," Mrs. Matthews says, taking her own phone from the counter and tapping it awake. "Read me his number, I'm going to text him mine so that he can get in touch with both of us."

I do so, my voice coming out robotic. It feels like I'm having an out of body experience, like I'm looking down on this scene from above as it happens to someone else.

"Okay." Mrs. Matthews puts her phone back on the counter and gives me a little nod. "The absolute worst thing that we can do right now is stand around and think about how bad things are. We need to get moving, stay active. Let's start some dinner together and then we'll eat, okay?"

I nod, even though I already know that there's no way I'm going to be able to choke down a single bite. Even the thought of sushi, which is my absolute favorite, is enough to turn my stomach. How in the world am I supposed to eat when my dad is sitting under arrest at the police station?

"Listen," Mrs. Matthews says, taking me by the arms and looking me in the eyes. "I know where your head's at, Lilah. You're starting to spiral, but you have to stop it. Letting your thoughts get away from you right now won't help your dad and it certainly won't help you. Okay?"

"Okay." I force the word out and then lean forward, letting her wrap her arms around me. "How long do you think until we hear something? It shouldn't be too long, right? I mean, he's innocent, so they should be able to figure that out pretty quickly and get this wrapped up and him back home to us, yeah?"

"I hope so." She squeezes me tight and then steps back to look at me. "Unfortunately, or I guess fortunately, Lilah, I don't have any experience with this sort of thing. As much as I'd love to be able to give you a solid answer on when I think that we'll see your dad again, I have no idea. All we can do is keep on keeping on, all right? I'm here."

My chin wobbles. "I know."

"And I'm not going anywhere. Right now, keeping you safe and making sure that you're going to be okay is the most important thing in the world to me. Nobody could tear me away from you right now, Lilah. You have to believe that."

I nod, tears brimming in my eyes. "This is going to sound crazy," I tell her, taking in a shaky breath, "but you feel like more than just my teacher." I don't know what I'm saying but I can't stop myself. It feels right to say this to her, especially after all that we've been through and what we're going through right now.

She tilts her head a little to the side as if waiting for me to continue.

"I didn't know my grandparents," I say, barging ahead, "but I'd like to think that they would have been something like you. And I know that you're not family, Mrs. Matthews, but sometimes it feels like you are. Like when you're teaching me things about plants in the woods or when you're helping me cook in the kitchen. It feels like you're the grandmother that I never had."

My cheeks blaze with fire, but I'm happy to have it off my chest. This is something that I've been thinking for a few days now. She'd mentioned before that she thought of me like a granddaughter, and it just feels really good to let her know how I feel about her. Even with my dad arrested for murder, I want to let her know how much she means to me and how much I appreciate her looking out for me.

"Lilah," she says, and I feel myself cringe. She's going to tell me that I'm crazy or that I need to get my head on straight because we're not related and won't ever be.

But she doesn't. Instead, she cups my cheeks, tilting my face up to look at her. "I never had the chance to be a grandmother, but Lilah, you are exactly who I would want as my granddaughter. I feel the same way. You feel like family."

I throw myself into her arms and she hugs me tight. Even though part of me feels bad having this talk while my dad is facing the worst day of his life, I can't help it.

I've wanted to feel like I belong to other people so badly for such a long time now. After losing my mom, my dad and I didn't really make connections with other people. I haven't had anyone like Mrs. Matthews in my life before, someone who honestly cares about me and enjoys spending time with me.

I swallow hard. "It's like you were put here in my life right when I needed you the most."

"I feel the same way, darling," she says, and I exhale hard in relief.

The despair eating into the back of my mind disappears a little bit and I sink into her arms. If I were on my own right now, I know that I couldn't possibly handle any of this. There's no way that I'd be able to face the thought of being here alone without my dad while he's talking to the police.

The thought of him going to trial would be even worse.

Things are still terrible, no matter how you look at them, but at least now I have someone in my corner. I'm not going to have to face whatever comes next by myself. I miss my dad and I want him home here with me more than anything, but at least Mrs. Matthews is here for me.

Thank goodness.

"Okay," she says, after a moment. "Let's see about what we want to make for dinner. I didn't really have anything in mind, so speak up if there's something that you're craving. Maybe a favorite comfort food?"

"Mac and cheese," I say without thinking. It was the one thing that my mom always made when she was stressed out. Of course, the type of mac and cheese that she made came in a box with an envelope of powdered cheese, and I have a feeling that that isn't going to fly with Mrs. Matthews.

"I think that I saw some bacon in the back drawer," she says, tapping her chin. "How about we do a smoky bacon mac and cheese with as many different kinds of cheeses as we can find in the fridge?"

My stomach growls at just the suggestion and she smiles

at me, touching me lightly once more on the cheek. "I promise you, Lilah, I'm here for you. No matter what."

"Thank you," I whisper, but she's already turned away and is pulling everything that we're going to need out of the fridge. Part of me is surprised that she's okay with me eating just pasta for dinner, but she obviously sees that this is what I need right now and she's more than happy to give it to me.

After a moment, I walk over and get out a pot to put some water on to boil. We work in silence, both of us lost in our own thoughts, but it doesn't matter that we don't speak. The two of us are connected as we move through the kitchen around each other and don't need words.

I heavily salt the water like she's shown me in the past and get down a glass jar of dry pasta. While I wait for the water to come to a rolling boil, I watch her work. She grates cheese quickly, like she's been doing it every day of her life, and then chops up the bacon, putting on a pan to cook it.

It's strange, even though she's only been here for a short period of time, it feels like she's been here forever. Already I can't imagine what my life would be like without her in it.

CAROL

*W*ell, well, well. The fantastic Doctor Grey Bennett didn't make bail.

I knew that he wouldn't. No judge in their right mind would let anyone accused of four murders out on bail, especially if they had anywhere near as much money as he does. He could easily flee the country, take Lilah with him, and start a fresh life away from the accusations waiting him here.

After the lawyer called and spoke to me, I relayed the information to Lilah. She hadn't wanted to go to bed until she got news about her dad. Even though it was well past her bedtime, I relented, but just this once.

Going forward, I'm going to be running this house the way that it should be run. No more catering to her when she's moody, no more allowing her to get her way all the time. She needs an adult who cares about her but is also willing to put their foot down when necessary, and that's me.

"Tell me again what evidence they have against him," Lilah says. She's halfheartedly poking at the oatmeal I made her for breakfast. It's loaded with chia seeds and hemp hearts, which will help fuel her brain today, but she's being incredibly stubborn and is refusing to eat it. Her hair is hanging limply around her face and she has huge bags under her eyes.

It's a good thing that I'm not planning on letting her leave the house today, because I don't want anyone to see her looking like that. It's one thing for her to look terrible when it's just her and her dad, but now that I'm here, she needs to look better. She just can't be walking around town looking like a drowned rat all the time. It would reflect badly on me.

"They found the same plant used to poison the men in the hospital garden," I tell her, and she shakes her head. I know what she's going to say, because she's said it half a dozen times now, so I cut her off. "And that wouldn't normally be enough to arrest him, but he eats lunch out there every day. They also found the plant here, growing in the back of your garden."

"I told you, I've never seen it there before," she argues, dropping her spoon to her bowl with a clatter. "I promise you, we never planted it."

Even though she's being a brat, I nod. "I know, darling, but someone did, because it was there. Maybe your dad did it when you weren't around, not knowing how dangerous it could be. Maybe it got planted by a gardener by accident. However it got there, it was there."

I still can't believe that the bumbling Detective Tanner couldn't find it on his own. He had an actual picture of the plant in his hand while looking for it, for goodness' sake, but no. They needed an anonymous tip to be called in before they were able to come back and find it. Ridiculous.

Lilah and I had been out of the house at the time, so she

never saw them poking around. I think that's why her dad's arrest was such a huge surprise to her. Not to me, although I did my best to act like it was.

Everything is going to plan. I killed the men, planted the salvia in the Bennett garden, and now I'm the only one who Lilah can depend on to take care of her.

I've always been great at planning. From the moment that I saw George, I knew that the two of us were going to be married. It took a little time before we got together, but once we did, nothing was going to tear us apart. I planned out our wedding and our lives together. The fact that it all came crashing down around my head thanks to Dr. Bennett was out of my control.

He's always been the one thing that I haven't been able to control, but now that he is going to be behind bars, I won't have to worry about him ever upsetting my life again.

"It just doesn't make sense." Lilah drops her head into her hands, pushing her bowl of oatmeal away from her decisively with her elbows. Even though I'm frustrated with her for not eating, I pick it up and quickly scrape the leftovers into the trash.

On any other day I would have made her finish it. I would have stood here over her until she ate every last bite and reminded her that wasting food is one of the worst things that you can do. But I'll go easy on her today. Technically I'm still just staying here as a favor to her dad.

When I'm given full custody rights over Lilah and the house, then I'll be able to really put my foot down about certain things. I certainly won't let her waste food.

"If you're not going to eat then we should probably get started with some math," I tell her calmly, taking her glass of juice and putting it in the refrigerator for later. "There's no reason for the two of us to just sit around and stare at each other. What's going to happen is going to happen. The two of us sitting around like bumps on a log won't do us any good."

Her eyebrows fly up in amazement. "You've got to be kidding me," she says, frowning a little. "My dad just got arrested for multiple murders and you want me to do math?"

"I know that it sounds harsh," I say, patting her hand, "but really the best thing for you right now is to keep your mind occupied. Just sitting and staring at the wall will make you go insane. Trust me, I know a thing or two about that."

She shakes her head doubtfully. "I don't know that I'm going to be able to concentrate."

I want to scream at her but I take a deep breath and count to ten before speaking again. "I know that it feels that way right now, Lilah, but trust me, once you get done with your math you'll be surprised at how fast the time has gone by. Besides, you want to take the test as soon as possible so that you can guarantee you're in the class with your friends in the fall, right?"

"Oo-kay," she tells me, stretching out the word. She gives her head a little nod, sniffing a bit as she does. I know that she's trying to pull herself together, no matter how hard that is.

"Why don't you go splash some water on your face and come on back?" I ask her. "I bet that will make you feel a lot better. We don't have to go at a breakneck pace or anything, but I do think a little routine will be a really good thing for you and will help you stop worrying about your dad all the time."

"I know, you're right," she tells me, standing up. "It's just that, after losing my mom, I can't have anything happen to my dad. He's always been there for me, always protected me and looked out for me, and it's crazy to think that he might not be able to do that for a while."

"Just for a while," I tell her. "I have no doubt in my mind that as soon as the detectives actually start doing their job that they'll realize that he's not the murderer. We just have to wait it out for a bit longer, okay?"

She gives me a wan smile and then leaves the kitchen. As soon as I hear her feet going up the stairs, I sigh, leaning back against the counter. I thought for a moment that she wasn't going to do what I wanted her to, and that's simply out of the question. Lilah has to learn that I'm in charge now.

She'll figure it out. She's not the brightest star in the sky, but I think that with a little training, Lilah will do just fine.

GREY

I know that I should call Lilah. Having Jeremy do it for me so that I didn't have to hear the fear, sadness and disappointment in her voice was a cowardly move and definitely not one that I'm proud of, but I honestly couldn't do it. It would have felt too much like the conversation we had when her mom and I sat her down to tell her about the cancer. How do you say that to a child as young as Lilah was?

Dropping my head into my hands, I squeeze my temples. How many times have I done this, wanting nothing more than to squeeze the memories out of my mind? Thinking about Sara brings a flood of mixed emotions every single time. Some of the memories are happy, when I remember our wedding day and how thrilled we were when Lilah was born.

But then my mind drifts to losing my wife and I have to take something to keep my head on straight. My shrink told me that there wasn't anything wrong with needing a little something to make it through really hard times, but I can't believe that I still rely on that little white pill. Sometimes it feels like it's the only thing keeping me from going off the deep end, and I hate myself for needing it.

A stronger man wouldn't need to take a pill like that. They wouldn't need to rely on it just to make it through the day. Even though I know that I shouldn't, sometimes I double up just to keep the loud roar in the back of my head at more of a bearable moan.

Good God, did I take too many and black out?

I pull my hands from my temple and look at them, slowly turning them over and over to see the fronts and the backs. Sara used to kiss my palms and tell me that it was a gift to be able to heal people the way that I do. She used to tell me that she admired how I could hold people's lives in my hands and bring them back from the brink.

But what if I held people's lives in my hands and, instead of pulling them back from death, pushed them towards it? Is that something that I'm even capable of? It can't be. Is being locked in this cell enough to make me feel like I'm already going insane?

"Bennett, lawyer here to see you." The guard outside my door looks like he hits the gym twice a day, before and after work. He flexes his arms a little bit when he catches me looking at him, like he's trying to warn me not to try anything stupid.

"Great," I say, standing up and wiping my hands on my pants. "Thank you." When he opens the door I walk through it, trying to keep my head held high. It's almost impossible in a place like this, where the paint is chipping off of the walls and everything smells vaguely of urine.

The man points me to a door at the end of the hall and I walk towards it, trying to fight the tension that I feel building. Surely if Jeremy were here to free me then the guard would have said that, right? Maybe not. Maybe Jeremy wants it to be a surprise for me. Whatever is going on, I'm just thrilled to be taking step after step towards that door and can't wait to hear what my old friend has to say.

Inside the room is a small wooden table with two chairs. Jeremy sits in one, bent over a file on the table, but he looks up when I walk in with the guard and immediately gets up to shake my hand. "How you holding up, Grey?" he asks, and I give my head a rueful little shake.

"Please tell me that you have good news," I say, sitting down in the chair across from him. There's a camera pointed at us in the corner of the room, the red light on it shining steadily to indicate that it's recording. There isn't any movement in the room. The door we walked through has been shut tightly behind us and there isn't a window for anyone to walk by or look in.

As far as rooms go, it's the barest one that I've been in in a long time. No rugs, lamps, or other tables decorate the space. The cinderblock walls are painted a dull gray, giving the whole space a closed-off and dark feel. Even the lights in the ceiling are too bright and cast unnatural shadows. The overall effect is a terrible combination of bright and drab.

"I'm sorry, but I don't," Jeremy says, after a moment. He looks up at me and then back down at the papers in front of him. "Toxicology is back on the first and second victims, but not the third yet. Looks like someone thought to run more advanced tests and they picked up salvia in the victims' systems, but you know that."

I nod. The detectives explained all of this to me in the interrogation room before. It hadn't made sense then and it still really doesn't now. "I don't know anything about salvia," I tell Jeremy.

"I know, but they found it growing in your garden and on the hospital grounds, so that's the evidence that they're using to tie you to the crimes. They thought about inter-viewing Lilah but ended up not doing so because of her age. She'd need a guardian there with her during questioning and with Sara gone and you locked up, that wasn't possible. Honestly, I think that they wanted to just move quickly and get you arrested, so they pushed really hard to find the salvia."

"How hard is really hard?" I put my hand flat on the table and lean closer to get a better look at my friend. "How hard exactly did they push to find the salvia, Jeremy?" My heart beats hard in my chest. We've all seen it on TV and read about it in the news—crooked cops who were willing to do anything that they had to, including fabricating evidence, just to get someone behind bars. "If they felt like they didn't need to talk to Lilah and were willing to arrest me for a plant that I swear wasn't growing in my garden, then how willing were they to make this happen?"

Jeremy eyes me for a moment. I'm sure that he's heard this from every single one of his clients before, but he knows me. He has to know that I'm serious, that I wouldn't do anything to jeopardize my life or Lilah's.

Then again, there's that voice in the back of my head telling me that maybe I did accidentally do something and I just don't remember it. The voice started out tiny, but it's getting louder.

"I'm sure you realize that I hear this from everyone," Jeremy says, picking up his folder and tapping some papers together in it. "But I really have no reason to believe that you're trying to pull one over on me, Grey." He pulls a photo from the folder and holds it out to me.

"Salvia, right?" I say, taking it. "Detective Laite had a similar photo last night and wanted me to look at it. I've never grown it, I swear. Besides, what's the supposed motive?"

"They think that you just snapped, that you couldn't handle the fame that comes with being the best cardiologist in this part of the state. That you want to go back to an easier time in your life, with your wife at your side."

"Well, they're right about that last part. I miss Sara. But surely that's not a crime. What else do they have?"

He pulls out photos of the four victims and shows them to me. "I want you to think long and hard about if you ever, *ever*, had any altercations with them or their families, because the detectives will overturn every stone possible in order to find any shred of evidence of you not getting along with them. It's best to come clean about it now if there's anything there."

"There's nothing." I shake my head. "I promise you, Jeremy, when I'm seeing a patient we don't talk about politics or anything else that would set us off. We just...do the thing. Save their life. Move on with mine. You know?"

"I figured as much. Well, then we need to establish your alibi. I'm assuming that Lilah will have been home with you on those nights, but they don't seem to care about her. We have to show, without a shadow of a doubt, that you couldn't have snuck by her without her noticing. It has to be so painfully obvious that nothing they think they have will stand up in court."

The dead men stare up at me from the table and I put the photos in a pile then hand them over to Jeremy. "Let's do it. I have to get this over with and home to Lilah."

"Speaking of which," he says, pulling out a tape recorder and putting it on the table between us. "Who is she with? Is DSS going to have to get involved?"

I shake my head, for the first time feeling relaxed and

comfortable with what's happening. Everything else may feel like it's falling apart, but at least I know that my daughter will be safe and taken care of. "She's with a friend, her math teacher," I say. "Carol Matthews. Moved in for a bit while she's dealing with a pretty nasty divorce."

Jeremy nods, then and raises one eyebrow but doesn't say anything at first. After a pause, he does. "And you trust her?"

"Oh, completely," I say instantly. "If Lilah can't be with me then Carol is the next best thing."

LILAH

I still haven't talked to my dad. I know that Mrs.
Matthews has, or at least to his lawyer, more than
once. She'll take a call then get a funny look on her face and
disappear from the room. When I ask her about it, she tells
me not to worry, that my dad is doing everything he can to
get home as soon as possible and all we need to do is work
hard here so that when he does come home, he can effort-
lessly slip back into his normal life.

But I don't know if that's going to be possible. I saw the
newspaper on the counter this morning. My dad's face
stared up at me from the front page like he was some
common criminal, and the headline was enough to make me
sick. They're calling him *Doctor Death*. I just hope that he
has no way of seeing the paper so that he won't know what
people are saying about him.

Of course, there were reporters camped out in front of
our house all this morning. Mrs. Matthews went out and
chased them away, but since then, we've had all of the
curtains drawn in the house. It's just best that way, or at

least, that's what she says. I can't say that I blame her, not with cameras pointed at our house and people ringing the bell all the time to try to talk to me.

Mrs. Matthews had promised me that doing math would take my mind off of things, but it didn't, not really. After finishing my work with her I disappeared into my room to read, except for when I had to come out to eat lunch and dinner. I don't even want to cook right now, I'm so upset.

Rolling over on my bed, I glance at the time on my phone. It's almost eleven pm, which means that she is in bed. She likes to go to bed at ten, saying that that gives her plenty of time to fall asleep before anything bad happens outside, whatever that means. I have literally no idea what type of bad things she could be talking about.

Unless she's talking about my dad getting arrested for murder.

My laptop emits a soft glow when I open it and I glance nervously at my door. It's dark out in the hall, so when I came up for bed, I pushed a hoodie up against the crack under my door so that no light could get through to the hall.

The last thing that I need is for Mrs. Matthews to come in here and tell me to get off of my computer. She's great, for sure, but I have some things that I feel that I have to do, like reading the newspaper articles being written about my dad. Once she realized that I saw the paper with his picture dad on the front, she took it away and hid it somewhere.

I have to figure out a way to show everyone that he's innocent.

The first article I click on makes my stomach churn by the second paragraph.

Known for being the most beloved cardiologist that this area has ever seen, Dr. Grey Bennett has touched the lives of many patients in wonderful ways. Unfortunately, the truth is just now coming out about how he may be touching their lives in terrible ways, as well. After the deaths of four of his past patients, Dr. Bennett is under arrest and being held in the county jail, where he will stay until his trial. His lawyer, Jeremy Alexander, maintains his client's innocence, but many in the town aren't so sure.

I click the back button. I don't think that I can stomach reading what people in town have to say about my dad. The same people who knock on his door whenever they have a medical problem now appear happy to throw him under the bus when it serves them.

The next article speculates whether or not my dad snapped after losing my mom. It claims that I've been abandoned at home, left to fend for myself, and it is only through the kindness of my math teacher stepping in that I'm not starving while my dad is in jail.

"Vultures, all of them," I mutter to myself, clicking back again out of the article. I don't know what I'm looking for, but I don't think that I'm going to find anything by reading these articles all talking about how terrible a person my dad is and letting them get me all riled up. There has to be some evidence out there that will help me find the real killer.

It's obvious that the detectives aren't going to keep the investigation open with my dad locked up, so I'll have to keep looking myself. I have to be the one to find the real killer and make sure that my dad doesn't go to jail. I hover the mouse over my bookmarks, debating whether or not I want to go down this particular rabbit hole. Before I can stop myself, I click on the first link.

It's a message board for true crime junkies. My dad and I discovered it some afternoon when reading up on one of the true crime documentaries that we'd watched together the night before. Anyone can post on it, about anything. Not only do people talk about their theories of what may have really happened with a crime, they also love showing off old photos of the victims and criminals. After we accidentally saw pictures that hadn't ever been released to the public, my dad had forbidden me from coming to this site again, and I'd obeyed him.

But now is not the time to continue to be a good girl. Someone has to figure out who really killed these guys and I run a search on my dad's name, my stomach churning as I type it into the search bar.

Grey Bennett.

The computer thinks for a moment before the screen refreshes. Only one hit appears and I click on it, noting that it was posted today. Whoever wrote it must be local, because I can't imagine that news of this case would have spread very far yet. The poster uses TruthFinder as their handle and the green circle next to their name tells me that they're online right now.

My palms are wet and I wipe them on my pajama pants as I start to read. It's only a few paragraphs, and all of them are short and pithy, but the gist is that TruthFinder doesn't believe that my dad killed his patients, either. I know that it's stupid, but I click on their name and fire off a message before I can stop myself.

Hi, TruthFinder, what makes you so sure that Dr. Bennett didn't kill his patients?

My name is YellowCat, which doesn't make sense, because I hate the color yellow and I'm allergic to cats, but my dad had told me that my name couldn't be anything that could possibly be tied back to me. He'd helped me come up with the name, saying that it was perfect because it was so unlike me.

OMG, Have you met him? He's the best. He operated on my dad a few years ago and my parents love him. They're in shock. Do you think that he did it? The words pop up on my screen with a soft *ping* and I quickly mute my computer. I have no idea how deeply Mrs. Matthews sleeps, but the last thing I need right now is for her to hear the sound and come check on me. Chances are very good that she wouldn't be happy that I'm on the computer trying to find my dad's killer right now.

Or that I'm talking to a stranger.

Not a chance. He's innocent, but then who did it? And why aren't the police looking harder?

I hate talking to random people online, but I'll do anything to help my dad. I'll spend all night talking to strangers if I can find any proof that he is innocent. I just hope that this person actually knows something and can be useful.

Those are good questions. It's possible that someone is framing him and doing a really good job. I wonder if he has any enemies.

"Does my dad have any enemies?" I whisper to my silent room. I know that I'm not going to find an answer in here, but I still look around like I fully expect something to jump out at me. Everyone loves him, and he's never complained about not getting along with people, but there must be someone he doesn't see eye-to-eye with.

Doubtful. Who would you look for?

I only have to wait a moment for TruthFinder to respond.

Someone with something to gain.

We talk for a bit longer before I'm so exhausted that I know I need to get some sleep. Even after I say goodnight and close up my laptop to lie down, though, I can't turn off my brain.

Someone with something to gain.

Everyone has something to gain from hurting someone else, but who in the world would have enough to gain from hurting my dad that they'd be willing to kill for it?

CAROL

*I*t's well past the time that she should be up and out of bed, but Lilah still hasn't come down for breakfast. Yesterday I took time to explain to her just how important it is for her to stick to a routine right now, and I really thought that she understood and agreed. It's something I was taught when I was a little girl: routine is the most important thing because it can keep you on track for every other part of your life.

But here it is, already almost seven in the morning, and I haven't heard a single bump or thump from her room. I want her to have autonomy, but she obviously needs me to be more of a mother figure than I thought at first. Slowly, I walk up the stairs and down the hall to her room.

Knocking once on the door, I wait for her to respond, but when she doesn't, I push the door open. She's sound asleep, curled up under her covers like a huge lump. I glance at her for a moment, but it's not her pile of blankets that really catches my eye. It's the laptop on her bed by her feet.

She was up late last night on the computer and now

she's sleeping past when she should be eating breakfast. I feel a tickle of anger building at the base of my spine and even though I want to ignore it, I stalk quietly across her room and grab her laptop.

It's sleek, new, definitely a gift from her dad. When Lilah still doesn't move, I set it on her desk and gently lift it open. There's a prompt for a password, which gives me pause. What kind of code would a girl like Lilah use to protect her secrets? And what kind of secrets would she have worth protecting?

My eyes fall on the corkboard above her desk. I hate corkboards, most of the time they're so messy and cluttered. Lilah's is no exception. She has photos tacked to the board, lists of phone numbers, even a calendar. I notice that she stopped crossing off the days two weeks ago.

Ugh. So messy. So unorganized. In such serious need of my help.

In all of the clutter, though, is a small pink sticky note. It's half hidden behind a photo of Lilah and some other girl, both wearing bikinis that shouldn't be worn by anyone young enough that they're still on their parents' health insurance. Curling my lip, I push the photo to the side to see what's written on the sticky.

Four digits. 4258.

Tapping it in, I grin as her screen lights up. Looks like Lilah was on the internet last night and was simply too tired to log out of whatever she was looking at. I'm curious to see what she thinks is so much more important than getting a good night's rest. Quickly, I skim the page, then have to work to hold back a gasp.

She's been on a message board for true crime. More than that, she'd been talking to someone about her dad and his case.

I glance over at her to make sure that she's still asleep. She hasn't moved an inch, which means that she must have been up really late last night. The timestamp on the last message that she sent saying that she was going to bed shows it was a little after midnight.

My hand shake as I scroll up to the beginning of the conversation. How Lilah could go behind my back like this is beyond me. Her father obviously trusts me to live in the house while he's gone and take care of his daughter, now she's up at all hours of the night sending messages to a stranger. Such audacity. She obviously thinks that she's gotten away with it, too. That makes me really angry.

Grabbing the laptop from her desk, I carry it carefully out of her room. Her door is open behind me, but I don't care if she wakes up right now. All that matters is that I get a chance to look at these messages and see what she and her online friend have said to each other.

After carrying the laptop downstairs, I pour myself a cup of coffee before settling in to look at it. It's bad enough that she went behind my back like this, sneaking around in the middle of the night and talking to someone else.

But what honestly worries me the most is the thought that she might have found out some information that I've been trying to keep secret. So far, it looks like she was only on this one site last night, but I have to make sure that she wasn't looking me up. If she did, then she'd be able to find out the truth about my past, and that simply can't happen. It would be—problematic, let's call it that.

I hold my breath when I click on her history to check if she was looking at anything else. It looks like this site was the only one that she was on last night, and I exhale hard in relief. It's still not great that she's poking her nose in where she shouldn't, but at least I know that she hasn't been looking into me.

I consider in my mind how I am going to stop her from doing something like this again, then shut the laptop and turn it over. Aha. Perfect. As nice as it is, it's not one with a solid base that would require screwdrivers to access the battery. There's a small compartment on the back that houses it and I easily flip off the cover and pop out the battery before snapping the cover back on.

Once that's done, I take the battery and tuck it into the trash under some coffee grounds, then walk carefully back up the stairs. Lilah's still sound asleep and doesn't move when I put the laptop back on her bed. This time, though, instead of leaving her room as quietly as I entered it, I lightly touch her shoulder.

"Lilah, darling," I say, giving her a small shake. "I made bacon and it's waiting for you downstairs. You okay, hon?"

She groans and rolls over, rubbing her eyes before looking at me. "Have you heard from my dad?"

Anger flares in me. I'm doing everything that I can for this ungrateful child. I've cooked her breakfast, made sure that she won't be tempted again by someone telling her lies on the internet, and have completely upended my life to take care of her, and the first thing that she asks about is her *dad*? How dare she?

"I haven't," I say, biting back the vitriol I feel. "But like I said, breakfast is downstairs waiting on you. Why don't you get up and we'll get this day started?"

"I don't want to eat," she says, tugging the covers up to her chin. "I don't know that I can without knowing for sure what's going to happen to my dad."

I stare at her, trying to keep myself calm. In school I have to keep my temper, because you're not allowed to really punish kids properly. Sure, you can take away their cell phones and make them stay after school, but if they talk back and are rude to you, you just have to grin and bear it.

I always did my best to make sure that the kids in my classroom weren't spoiled, and I promised myself that any child I dealt with would have manners. Here's my chance to put that into action. Lilah is spoiled, but she doesn't have to be a lost cause.

"You need to eat to keep up your strength," I tell her, tugging down her blankets. She's so surprised that she lets go of them and they slip easily from her grip. "Besides, I made you food. Don't be rude and stay in bed when someone has done something nice for you. Starving yourself isn't going to help your dad. Do you think that he's starving himself so that you'll feel better?"

Tears brim in her eyes but I honestly don't care. Crying over something as trivial as this is just a sign of weakness. If Lilah's going to make it in the world then she needs to learn how to pull herself together, starting now.

"Get up," I tell her, turning and walking from the room. "You need to be downstairs for breakfast in ten minutes, do you understand?"

She doesn't answer. I don't really expect her to. When you haven't been raised with any manners then it probably comes as quite a surprise to suddenly be asked to have some. That's fine. She'll go through a little adjustment period, but after that, everything is going to be so much better.

LILAH

"What is that woman's problem?" I ask, gritting my teeth before trying to kick my legs over the side of my bed to get up. My sheet is wrapped around them and I flail for a moment before freeing myself.

But not before I hear the dull thud of my laptop hitting the floor.

"No," I whisper, my heart in my mouth, slipping from my bed and dropping to my knees next to it. "Please, be okay. I need you to be okay." My fingers shake a little as I open it up. The screen doesn't light up and I press the ESC button a few times.

Nothing. The screen remains as black as ever. I try Ctrl+Alt+Del over and over, hoping that that will bring it back to life. Each time I hit those three keys, I have renewed hope that it will spring back to life. It doesn't.

The tears that I'd been trying so hard to hold back while Mrs. Matthews was in here now burst free and fall down my cheeks. I don't try to stop them, not even when some of them splash onto the trackpad. I can't believe it. I was working on my computer so hard last night to try to clear my dad and now suddenly it doesn't even work.

Sitting back against the bed, I close the laptop, trying to hang onto some of the hope that I was feeling last night. I honestly thought I was making some good progress in helping my dad. No, I don't have a suspect, and no, I haven't uncovered any clues that the detectives missed, but still.

It also felt really good to talk to someone else who believes that my dad is innocent. TruthFinder obviously thinks like I do: that something terrible is happening to my dad, that he's getting framed, and that the police don't seem to care. That's the worst part, that it doesn't seem to matter to them that my dad is innocent.

As my new friend said last night when we were signing off, "As long as the police put someone behind bars and nobody else dies, then what do they care if they got the right person or not?"

I drop my head into my hands and try to remember. There was something else that they said last night that really made me stop and think. What was it?

The smell of bacon wafting through the open door reminds me that Mrs. Matthews wants me downstairs for breakfast. As much as I'd like to sit on the floor and try to remember what TruthFinder said, I get up and pull some clothes from my dresser. I change without really paying attention to what I'm doing, then pick my laptop up from the floor.

That's weird, I think to myself. The laptop feels incredibly light and I turn it over, looking for anything amiss. Everything looks fine, but I'd swear in court that something was not right with it. Never in my life have I felt a laptop that feels this light.

Sitting down on the edge of my bed, I flip my laptop

over and run my fingers along it. Everything feels fine. There's a small dent on one edge where it slammed into the floor when it fell, but that wouldn't explain why it feels like it's a pound or two lighter.

That may not sound like a lot, but when you're dealing with a laptop, two pounds can make a huge difference. I know that it's silly, because it was working just fine last night, but still I pop off the battery compartment.

It's empty.

I suck in a breath, trying my best to fill my lungs so that I don't accidentally pass out. There's no way that my battery could be missing, but it's gone. My fingers dip into the compartment where it goes and I run them around the edge, trying to puzzle through what must have happened.

There's absolutely no way that it could have just fallen out. I also know that there's no way on earth that I would have removed it. That doesn't make any sense, no matter how you look at it. The problem is, the only other possibility is that Mrs. Matthews took my battery.

But why on earth would she do that? She would have had to have come in while I was asleep and taken it on purpose. Everyone knows that kids have computers in their rooms, so why would it be a big deal?

Then I remember what TruthFinder had said to me. When I asked them who you would look for as a suspect, who my dad had as an enemy, I hadn't been able to think of a single person. But my new anonymous online friend had had a simple answer for me, one that made me feel sick to my stomach last night, and makes me want to throw up now that I remember it this morning.

Someone with something to gain.

That's what they had said, and at the time, I pushed it out of my mind. Nobody wants to hurt my dad, and I can't think of a single person who would have something to gain by putting my dad behind bars.

A terrible realization dawns on me, one that I'm certain I shouldn't even entertain. My dad would be pissed if he thought that I was thinking what I am. And yet...

There's only one person who would have had access to my laptop since I was on it last night. I know that I'm a heavy sleeper, that's something that my dad has always told me. But do I really sleep so soundly that Mrs. Matthews could come into my room and take my laptop out to look at it without me waking?

I'm not sure. Turning the laptop over in my hands again, I get up and put it back on my desk where it belongs. Part of me wants to rush downstairs right now and confront Mrs. Matthews about what's going on, but there's another part of me that's terrified to do so. What if I'm wrong?

I want to believe that I'm being ridiculous, that there's no way on earth that Mrs. Matthews would have taken my battery, but I have to face the facts.

Unless I'm suddenly a sleepwalker, or someone else broke into the house for the express purpose of taking the battery from my laptop, she's the only other person who had access to it. As much as I don't want it to make sense, she's the only person who could have taken the battery.

But why?

My eyes fall on my phone, which is plugged in to charge during the night as it always is. It's on my desk but there's a piece of paper that's been shuffled to cover it up. I wonder if she would have taken it had she noticed it sitting there. I push that thought from my mind and remove it from its charger, swiping the screen to turn it on.

Once it wakes all the way up, I tap on my email to see if I have any new messages. The website I was on last night sends out emails if you sign up for notifications on certain posts, and I'm hoping that someone will have written something helpful on the post about Dad.

There's a new message on the post about him, just one, and I hold my breath while I click on it. The page takes a moment to load and I have to log in first, which is frustrating when all I want to do is read what they wrote. After a moment, though, the page loads, and I let my eyes flick down the screen.

As soon as I do, my heart sinks. TruthFinder honestly seems to believe that my dad is innocent of these murders. From what they wrote here and what they said privately to me yesterday, they believe that he's innocent and should be home with me right now while the police try to find the real killer.

But this new user doesn't agree. Their entire long, rambling post is them congratulating the police on a job well done. Please. As if the police actually even read these boards. My stomach churns and I turn the phone off, ready to drop it onto my desk.

And then I remember the laptop battery and I pause, holding the phone to my chest for a moment. If Mrs. Matthews was willing to take my laptop battery so that I couldn't use my computer, then I have no reason to think that she won't take my phone as well. I feel a little silly doing it, but I tuck my phone in behind my bras in my dresser and make sure that it's not visible.

Maybe that's insane, but right now, I feel more than a little crazy. I also feel like I have to be careful. I'm one of the only people who seems to be trying to help my dad and I can't lose my way of contacting the outside world.

My heart is pounding as I walk out of my room, but I do my best to keep my face still and straight as I head down the stairs. Mrs. Matthews has no reason to believe that I suspect her of anything. If she really is the person who wants to keep my dad in jail for some reason, then I have to be careful. I can't, under any circumstances, let her know that I have any inkling what she's up to.

CAROL

By the time Lilah finally deigns to make an appearance at breakfast, I'm well and truly frustrated. I honestly thought that by moving in here I'd be able to whip her and this house into shape in no time. It would be easy if she weren't already so badly trained to be sloppy and rude.

Grey Bennett may be worshipped as a god in the operating room, but his daughter is sassy, and that needs to change. I'm fully expecting a fight when she finally walks into the kitchen, especially if she tried to get on her computer first thing this morning, but she just gives me a cheery 'good morning' and sits down at the counter, resting her chin in her hand.

"Sorry I'm so late getting downstairs," she says. "When I push myself too hard I sleep like the dead when I finally collapse. I think that everything that's been going on recently just finally caught up with me. Breakfast smells amazing, thank you." She gives me a small smile and I feel a bit of my anger wane away.

She's not a bad kid, she's just had terrible guidance for

most of her formative years. That's over now, though, thank goodness. I just have to make sure that she understands that I'm the boss and then I'm sure that we'll get along just fine.

I serve her some breakfast and then sit next to her, watching as she digs in and noting that I still need to break her of that awful bacon habit. Part of me was curious if she'd discover that I took her laptop battery last night, but it's obvious from the way that she's digging right into her food that the thought hasn't even crossed her mind. If she had tried to get onto her computer this morning without any luck then I'm pretty sure that I'd be able to tell.

"So I want to get back into a good routine today," I tell her. "While you're working on math I'll call your dad's lawyer and see if there are any updates in the case. I think that it's good to stay informed, but there has to be a balance. There's no reason for us to be checking in with him multiple times a day. That will only lead to you getting upset if things are moving too slowly."

She nods, swallowing, then drinks half of her coffee in one go before speaking. "Okay, but I do want to talk to him myself today. I'm sure that he'll want to ask me some questions, and I'd like to get that scheduled and out of the way."

I fold my hands in my lap and purse my lips. Children aren't supposed to talk back to adults, and they're certainly not supposed to try to get what they want when someone is doing everything they can for them. Lilah would know that by now, if her parents had ever bothered to teach her manners. But I guess like so many parents these days they relied on computers and the television to raise their child. No surprise that Lilah ended up talking back and thinking that she knows what's best for her.

"I doubt that he'll want to do that so soon in the process," I tell her. "If Mr. Alexander wants to speak with you then I'll make a time that he can come by the house. Trust me, I'm going to do what is best for you and your dad while also making sure that you're not too exposed to everything that's going on."

For a moment, I think that she's going to argue with me. Her cheeks flush a little bit and it looks like she's trying to hold back something that she wants to say to me. I almost dare her to spit it out, to let me know what she's thinking. Part of me wants to really show her that she can't speak out against me, but the other part of me is impressed.

She obviously wants to say something, but is doing her best to keep it in.

"Thank you, Mrs. Matthews," she finally says. Her words are clipped, forced, but I don't care. As long as Lilah understands that I'm the only one who can help her, then she'll become a much better listener, I'm sure of it.

"Happy to help," I say, reaching out and patting her on the shoulder. "It's never a good thing for someone your age, no matter how bright, to take on more than they can handle. I know that you want to be involved in everything, Lilah, but I'm here to protect you. Let me do that and I promise you that you'll get through this a lot easier than you would otherwise."

For a moment, she just stares at me. I'm almost certain that she's going to argue with me or tell me that she hates me, but a small smile touches her lips. Good. As strong-willed as she is and as tough as she's trying to act, Lilah is just like any other kid her age who hasn't ever had someone take control for her.

She craves someone to make her life easier, and I'm here to be that for her. Teenagers especially, I have found, need someone to step in and take charge of what's going on for them. They want to have someone who will keep them insulated from all of the hard challenges in life.

I can be that person for Lilah, and I think she is realizing that. I'm going to do everything in my power to make her life as wonderful as possible. Unfortunately for her and her dad, that means separating the two of them. Grey Bennett is unfit to be a father. I'm protecting Lilah from him by stepping in, and I'm sure that eventually she'll be able to see that.

"Thank you," she whispers. "I had no idea how hard this would be. It's so much easier with you here to help me."

See? I knew that she'd come around.

"I'm so glad," I say. nodding back at her breakfast. "Now, eat up, Lilah, then we'll get started on our day. I think that you'll quickly learn that getting going in the morning is the best way to ensure that you have a wonderful rest of your day. No dilly-dallying in bed or at the breakfast table. An efficient start makes for a great day."

"Yes, Mrs. Matthews," she says.

A thought occurs to me. "You know, Lilah, you told me that you thought of me as a kind of grandmother before. I don't want you to feel any pressure, but you should feel free to call me something other than Mrs. Matthews if you'd like to. We're obviously closer than a teacher and a student, especially now that we're going through this together."

She's listening closely and for once doesn't interrupt to tell me what she thinks. Good. A girl her age is much better seen than heard and I'm tired of her constantly putting in her two cents.

"I know that you weren't ever close with your grandparents, so I want to give you the choice of what you want to call me. You can call me something like Grandma, or Nona, or even just Honey." I read that in a book once, where the grandchildren called their grandmother 'Honey'. All my life I've wanted to have kids call me that, but I've also always known that it probably wasn't going to happen.

"I like Honey," she says, after a moment. "If that's okay with you. I know that you're my teacher, but you do feel like you're something more than that."

"Honey is wonderful," I tell her, and actually smile at her for real. When she's not being insufferable, I think that I could get to like the girl. She just has to learn that she's not in control all the time, and has to listen to me and behave, and then we're going to get along just fine.

"Honey," she says, like she's trying it out. "Okay. I think that's good. You're right, you're more than just a teacher." For a moment, she just smiles at me, then she looks down at her plate. "I'm sorry, but I don't think that I can eat much more right now. My appetite is all messed up with every-thing that's been going on. May I please be excused to brush my teeth?"

I'm so delighted that I'd clap my hands together if I didn't think it would scare Lilah off. If she were younger I'd tell her how proud I am of her for remembering her manners right now, but instead I just give her a nod and a smile. "That's very mature," I say to her. "Why don't you do that and then come back down so that the two of us can get started on our day?"

"Sounds great." She stands and picks up her plate, but I stop her. If she's going to be making an effort to be a better person and to have nicer manners, then I'll make sure that she sometimes gets rewarded for it.

"I'll take care of the plate, darling," I tell her. "You just go on upstairs."

Lilah does what I tell her without responding, which is

amazing. I don't know why the doctor had such a hard time getting her to be polite. All it's going to take is a firm hand and a little time, and I'm going to turn her into a wonderful person. It'll be work at first, but I have no doubt that it'll all be worth it when everyone sees what an incredible job I've done with her.

LILAH

*A*s soon as I get into the bathroom I shut the door behind me and turn on the fan. My fingers grip the edges of the sink as I lean over it and stare into myself in the mirror.

"Honey," I sputter, then rinse my mouth with water, angrily spitting it into the sink. "She wants me to call her *Honey*?!"

The word feels disgusting in my mouth, cloying, overly sweet and sticky, and I don't ever want to say it again. I used it just now to make her think that I'm listening to her and doing what she wants, but that's the last time that I'll ever do it. For the rest of the time that she's here, I just won't call her anything to her face.

Hopefully, she won't be here very much longer. I don't know what her end goal is here, but she sure started striding around the house like she owned it as soon as my dad was in trouble. At first, it had been amazing. Knowing that I wasn't going to be alone in the house was wonderful, especially while the cops were nosing around, but I think that Dad and I made a huge mistake letting her stay.

On the other hand, I don't know where I could have gone. I'm too young to be on my own for a long time, I'm sure of that, and it's not like we have any family to step in and let me live with them.

Maybe a friend of my dad's. Someone from work, perhaps—

Cherry.

I realize with a thud that Cherry probably would have loved to help out and I feel tears sting the corners of my eyes when I think of her cheerful, bouncy personality. Angrily I wipe them away, then brush my teeth. I have to keep moving, keep doing what Mrs. Matthews wants, but at the same time I need to try to figure out what her end game is here.

She obviously doesn't want me to talk to Dad's lawyer. And it's also obvious that she wants to be head of the house. She wouldn't have taken my laptop battery if she wasn't trying to keep me under her control for some reason, either, though I have no idea why.

My electric toothbrush whirs in my mouth, and the two minutes run by quickly. Spitting, I start it back up again to buy another few moments alone, not wanting to go downstairs until I can really wrap my mind around what's going on.

I'm going to have to get some time by myself so that I can call the lawyer. I don't want to only hear what he's saying filtered through Mrs. Matthews. Before, I wouldn't have thought that she would ever lie to me about what he said, but now I'm not so sure. Now that she's stolen my laptop battery and asked me to call her Honey, I can't help but think that she isn't going to be totally honest with me about what's going on.

Spitting, I rinse and then splash some water on my face,

trying to look a bit happier and more alert. I always get terrible red circles under my eyes when I've been crying, even if it's only one tear. I've always hated that about me, but then my dad told me a few years ago that my mom was the same way.

I guess if I have to look a bit like a sad raccoon when I cry, I might as well look like that because it's something I get from my mom. At this point in my life, I feel like I'm scrambling for any way that I can be more like her. Sure, I remember her, but my memories are so faint and distant, and I was so young that I obviously didn't get to know her that well.

I have a feeling though, that were she still here she would know exactly what to do in this situation. My mom never backed down from a challenge, according to my dad. She also wasn't afraid to take on problems that were bigger than her if she thought that there was some injustice in the world that needed to be righted.

I want to be just like her.

Drying my face, I pull in a shuddering breath, then lift a small gold chain from next to the sink. It's not something that I wear very often because I'm always afraid that I'm going to break it, but right now I think that feeling it around my neck would be a comfort. I put it on and shiver as the cool gold hits my skin.

This is the necklace that my dad gave my mom when I was born. It's a simple chain and most people would say it wasn't a lot to look at, but my mom wasn't someone who liked overly showy stuff. She was happy with the simple things in life, and kind, and everything else that I want to be when I grow up.

Including ruthless when someone she loved was in trouble.

It feels like armor around my neck and I head back downstairs, ready for whatever the morning brings. Yes, I'll do my math with Mrs. Matthews, and I'll clean up around the house and be polite like she wants me to be, but as of today I also have my own agenda.

I'm going to get some time alone in my room to call Dad's lawyer. And I'm going to figure out as much as I can about my math teacher. She's going through a divorce, I know that much, but she's also still wearing a necklace that she told me came from the love of her life.

I've never even had a boyfriend, but I'm pretty sure that if I did, and he gave me jewelry, then abused me, I'd stop wearing it immediately. There's no way that I'd want that reminder anywhere near me, but I see Mrs. Matthews reaching up and touching it from time to time. I see the look in her eyes when she does. It's only there for the tiniest of flashes, but it's there.

She may think that I'm not paying attention, but I am, and I'm determined to figure out what she's really doing here. I don't believe in coincidences, which means that she's at my house for a reason, and I'm beginning to think that it's not all out of the goodness of her heart.

~

It's late in the morning by the time we finish math. We've never worked this long without a break and my hand is cramping from holding my pencil all morning. If I weren't slightly suspicious of Mrs. Matthews, I'd just dismiss it, but now it feels like she wants me to be occupied for as long as possible.

She slipped away from the kitchen table when I was graphing inequalities to go to the bathroom, but I noticed that she took her phone with her. She never goes anywhere without it now and even though she keeps it on silent, I feel like she's always checking it.

She's looking for something, or waiting for something, I'm not sure. No matter what it is, I'm also looking. Watching. Waiting.

It's obvious that she thinks that she's getting away with something. Fine, let her think that.

I'm onto her now.

CAROL

$\mathcal{M}$y conversation with Jeremy Alexander was less than useful. He honestly believes that Dr. Bennett is innocent, which I suppose he is of these murders, and also wants to talk to Lilah. I explained to him as patiently as possible that she's feeling much too fragile right now to discuss the details of her father's case, and he had the gall to tell me that the conversation wasn't optional.

When he told me that he was more than happy to come to the house to talk to her if I didn't want to bring her to him, I thought I'd fall out of my chair.

This man has to be twenty years younger than I am, and yet he honestly believes that I'm going to bend to his will and do what he wants. Well, that's not how this works. I'll bring Lilah by to meet with him, if he absolutely insists, but I have a plan on how this meeting is going to go.

"We'll be home before lunch," I promise Lilah as I back carefully down the driveway in my old beater. I did consider using Grey's car to take us to the lawyer, but I'll be driving his car soon enough. I'll look great driving a nicer car than this old one, that's for sure. And after all that I've been through, I deserve it.

There are just a few more things that I need to do first before I can get behind that wheel.

"Thanks for taking me," Lilah says, giving me a smile before settling back in her seat. I've driven her around many times before to get to our hiking locations. Normally she spends most of the time staring out of the window, but this time she turns to me. "I'm sorry, I've not checked in on you. That's rude. How are you doing?"

Her question is innocent enough but I still blink at the road and my hands tighten on the wheel imperceptibly. "With what, darling? Moving in with you? You know how happy I am to do it."

"Sure, but that's not what I mean. I meant with your husband. That's the reason you were staying with us in the first place, right?" Her tone is chatty and innocent and when I risk a glance at her, she has a very worried expression on her face.

"It is," I say, turning my attention back to the road. We're approaching a red light and I stop a safe distance from the car in front of me. How ironic it would be to get into a wreck on the way to meeting with the lawyer! "I haven't had any contact with my husband, so that's probably a good thing."

"He hasn't reached out to you?" She sounds surprised. So innocent, so stupid. It's no wonder that she was failing algebra.

I shake my head. "He's not allowed to, under the terms of the court order. No contact. If he does call or show up then he's going to get into trouble."

"Wow," she says softly. "You're so much braver than I am. If I were faced with something like that then I think that I'd have to pack up and leave town. I'd want to run and just put as much distance between me and him as possible. No reminders of him, nothing."

"It's better to be strong and stand up for yourself than run away from your problems." It feels good to be able to impart some wisdom to Lilah. I have no idea if it will stick or not, but she needs to hear that the world doesn't always work the way that you want it to. Privileged, spoiled Lilah. She's always had everything just given to her by her parents, but that's not how it's always going to be. Better that she figure it out now before the world crushes her later in life.

"But you didn't keep anything that reminds you of him, did you? I couldn't."

Why is she asking so many questions today? I glance over at her and, like she can read my mind, she hurriedly speaks again.

"I know that I'm being nosy, I'm sorry. I'm just trying to wrap my mind around what you're going through. I've been so caught up in everything with my dad that I guess I forgot that other people have troubles of their own."

"That's a sign of maturity, Lilah," I tell her. "I'm honestly impressed, and frankly didn't expect that from you. So often people get focused on what they're going through and think that their problems are the biggest ones in the world, but they're usually not. There's always someone out there who has it worse than you. And no, to answer your question, I didn't keep anything that would remind me of him. That's the last thing I'd want right now, isn't it?"

She nods. "Of course. You're totally right."

Good. Grey has only been out of the picture for a few days but already I'm making amazing headway with Lilah. I'm sure that with a bit more time I can mold her into the type of person who can actually be functional and productive. Right now, she still expects everything to be handed to her, but I'll take care of that attitude as quickly as possible.

We pull into a parking space in front of a dingy, squat building. There are weeds growing up through the sidewalk and the bushes out front are in desperate need of a trim. I never would have chosen to work with anyone who uses this place as their office, but until I get my hands on some of Dr. Bennett's money, this is all that I can afford.

"I have to run in here and get some paperwork for my divorce," I tell her. "You stay here, but don't touch anything. My poor little car is almost falling apart, as you know, and the last thing that I want is to have to pay for repairs. So hands in your lap, Lilah. Sit still. I'll be right back."

I shoot a glance at her over my shoulder before I enter the building. She's doing exactly what I told her to and sitting with her back ramrod straight, staring at me. I give her a little wave and she returns it, then drops her hand back into her lap.

Good. Hopefully this won't take too long and I can get in and out without her being locked in my car for too long. I guess that it wouldn't be a big deal to bring her inside with me and have her sit with the receptionist, but I want to be in complete control here. She needs to learn that I'm always going to do what's best for her.

And for me.

"I'm here to see Mr. Taylor," I say to the small receptionist right inside the front door. She smells like a smoker and has dyed red hair that needs to be retouched at the roots. Her natural dirty blonde is showing.

"Is he expecting you?" she asks, and I roll my eyes. I honestly don't have time for this, so I spin away from her rickety little desk and walk right into Mr. Taylor's office, knocking only once before pushing the door open.

He's at his desk, a Danish halfway up to his mouth, and his eyes widen when he sees me walk through the door. Good. I have no problem at all catching people by surprise, especially if that means that I'm going to get the results that I want faster.

"Good morning, Mrs. Matthews," he says, putting down his pastry and wiping his hands on a napkin. "I'm sorry, I didn't realize that you were coming in so early this morning."

"I hope that's not a problem," I say, looking past him out the window to the parking lot. I can just see the side of the car, but I can't see Lilah, so I move a few paces to the left until she comes into view. She's still sitting right where I left her.

Goodness, I didn't even think about the notebook in the console. I'm so used to keeping my list close to me at all times that it never crossed my mind to take it out of the car before Lilah got in.

What if she finds it?

Even as that fear threatens to take over, I do my best to push it out of my mind. Lilah isn't going to go poking around for something in my car. She's much too worried about her father to do something like that right now. In fact, she probably loves being told exactly what to do so she doesn't have to think about it.

"Not at all. Your husband signed the divorce papers, so we're good to go on that end." He takes a folder out of his desk drawer and puts it on his desk, giving it a little pat as he looks at me.

"And the...other matter?" I ask him, trying to keep from sounding too excited.

"Ah, yes, the question of custody. It's an interesting situation, Mrs. Matthews, as I'm sure that you're aware. I'm going to have to talk to Dr. Bennett himself and see if he will agree to sign the papers."

"He will," I tell him. I'm confident that Grey Bennett will want to do whatever he can to keep his daughter safe and protected. That's where I come in. "But I need more than just custody of her, Mr. Taylor. If I'm going to be able to keep her living in the manner to which she's become accustomed then I'm also going to need access to the doctor's accounts."

Mr. Taylor nods. At his heart, he's a slimy little man and I have no doubt that he is imagining the big paycheck in his future if this all works out the way I want it to. "Naturally. I'll speak to him about that as well. How quickly do you want that all taken care of?"

"Now." Why is it so hard for people to understand that I'm a woman of action and I need to get results in a timely manner? "I want it taken care of today so that I can make sure that Lilah has everything she needs. Figure it out, Mr. Taylor, and make sure that you get back to me as soon as possible."

LILAH

I've never met Mr. Alexander, but right now I can't wait to be alone in a room with him so that the two of us can talk about what's going on. Hopefully she won't take too long here at this other lawyer's and we'll get back on the road right away.

As soon as Mrs. Matthews disappears into the building, I pop open the glove compartment right in front of my seat. Of course I do. It falls open easily and I poke through the contents.

Registration, information about the car, warranties that expired ten years ago, a first aid kit, and a handful of paper napkins. That's all that she had in there, and they are all neatly arranged, like she cleans it out on a regular basis.

Judging from the overall condition of the car, I'd believe that.

The center console is much more interesting. I lift the top quickly and reach in to pull out a single notebook nestled on top of a pair of winter gloves. At first, I'm disappointed when I flip through it. I honestly don't care about her grocery lists or what errands she needs to run for the day, but when I reach the list of names on the center page, the top one crossed off, my blood runs cold.

I recognize them the moment I see them. They've been all over the news, in the paper, and whispered by my dad on the phone too many times for me to not know them immediately.

The first four names on Mrs. Matthews's list are the murder victims.

~

M r. Alexander walks into the conference room where the two of us are going to talk and sits down across from me. He's got a kind face and gives me a smile before he speaks. I was already on edge waiting for this meeting to get started, because I wanted to tell him that my dad is innocent, but now I also need to figure out what I saw in Mrs. Matthews's car.

It just doesn't make any sense. There's absolutely no way that she's the murderer, but why else would she have a list of those names written down in a notebook? Why would she have crossed the top name off it? And why would she lie to me about the necklace that she had on?

It might seem like a little thing to someone else, but it really struck me the way that she told me her necklace was from her "one true love". If that man is the same one she's divorcing now, then it doesn't make any sense to leave it on.

My head spins as Mr. Alexander pushes a piece of paper across the table to me. He hands me a pen and I click it three times to try to clear out some of my nerves.

"Hi, Lilah," he begins. His voice is so calming and soothing. "How are you today?"

I give my head a little shake and look right at him. I'm

suddenly unable to speak. My throat has closed up and even though I know that I need to be able to pull it together and talk to this man, I'm not sure that I can. Next to me, Mrs. Matthews shifts in her chair and she reaches out, putting her hand lightly on my arm to comfort me.

But all I can see in my mind's eye is her list in her car.

"I'm sorry, Mr. Alexander," Mrs. Matthews says, "but you can see just how much this is affecting Lilah. She's been having a hard time right now, as you can imagine."

"Completely understandable," he says, giving me a friendly smile. I want to talk to him about Dad, want to tell him what I saw in the car and ask him what he thinks it means, but I don't think that I can right now, even if I could get Mrs. Matthews out of the room to have some privacy. It honestly feels like all of the words that I'd want to say are stuck in my mouth and I can't seem to figure out how to say them.

"Unfortunately, I do need to talk to you, Lilah. The detectives are going to call you in for questioning, I'm sure, and I want to talk to you before they do that." When I don't answer right away, he glances over at Mrs. Matthews. "Do you think that Lilah is going to be able to handle questioning today?"

Mrs. Matthews still has her hand on my arm and gives it a little squeeze. Without meaning to, I look down at it and then up at her face. I don't like that they're having a conversation about me right in front of me, and I can't even seem to get involved.

"I think that Lilah is having a much harder time than she's been letting on," she says. "Please let Grey know, the next time you talk to him, that I'm with her and helping her through it all the best that I can."

"That's something I want to talk to you about." Mr.

Alexander glances over at me, obviously trying to gauge how well I'm handling things, then turns back to Mrs. Matthews. "Grey and I were talking about giving you custody of Lilah while he's in prison and facing this trial. It wouldn't be permanent, of course, but it would allow you to take care of Lilah while he was unable to. Of course, we know that that's a lot to ask..."

She sees the question hanging in the air and answers it immediately. "Well, of course she needs someone to look out for her. This is just so overwhelming." A slight pause, long enough to make me look over at her, then she continues. "Do you know a lawyer in town by the name of Taylor?"

Mr. Alexander nods, a frown creasing his forehead. "I do, slightly. Why? Is he getting involved with the case?"

Mrs. Matthews laughs and shakes her head, like she can't believe how silly he is. "He's not, but he's helping me with a different private matter and was going to talk to Grey himself about giving me custody of Lilah. I had no idea that we were all thinking the same thing, but it sounds like we are. It's wonderful to think that we're all trying to do what's best for Lilah here."

I turn to her with shock on my face. "You want custody of me?" I blurt out, unable to stop myself.

Mrs. Matthews smiles and pats my hand. "Lilah dear, someone has to look out for you, and your dad isn't going to be able to do that for a while. I just wanted Mr. Alexander here to be on the same page as us, but it sounds like he and your dad already are. That's a really good thing, because it means that we can all work together. Trust me, Lilah. This is good."

Trust her? I don't know how I possibly can. All I can see now when I look at her is the list I found in her car. Even though I know that it's probably insane, my mind won't let me stop thinking that she had something to do with the murders.

But that's nuts, right? She's a tiny little lady. She couldn't possibly overpower and kill a man.

But she could poison them.

"Lilah, darling, you look like you just saw a ghost. Are you okay?" Her voice is so kind that I can hardly believe I'm having these thoughts right now. Mr. Alexander hands her a piece of paper and she barely glances at it before signing it and passing it back across the table to him.

"Can I speak to you?" I finally find my voice and direct the question at Mr. Alexander, who looks a bit surprised at my request. "Um, alone?"

It feels strange to ask that sitting right next to Mrs. Matthews, but I need to know if I'm going crazy and seeing things that aren't there. I have to talk to someone about what's going on. I have to tell him about the list that I found in the car. There's no way that I'm going to do that with her sitting right next to me.

As of right now, she has no idea that I found it, and I definitely want to keep it that way for a bit longer.

"I'll be here with you," Mrs. Matthews says, but I don't look away from the man across from me. "Lilah," she says, squeezing my arm. "I'm here to be your support and guardian. That means you don't need to face any of this on your own."

"Alone," I plead, looking right at the lawyer. "*Please.*"

He gives his head a little shake and points at the piece of paper on his desk that he just had Mrs. Matthews sign. "Your guardian needs to be with you while you're being questioned, Lilah. You're underage."

"My guardian? You really made her my guardian just

now? Just like that? Don't I get a say in this?" I can't help the questions coming out of my mouth. I know that I should at least try to pretend to be happy about this, but I can't help it.

I should just blurt out what I suspect. If it's all out in the open then Mrs. Matthews can't hide from it, but oh boy, what if I'm wrong? I can only imagine how miserable my life will be.

"It's a good thing," Mrs. Matthews assures me, and Mr. Alexander nods. "A young girl like you shouldn't have to face what's going on without someone to look out for her, and I'm that person. I promise you, Lilah, nothing bad is going to happen to you. I'm here for you just like I was before, but now I'm legal in the eyes of the court. That's the only difference."

"This is a smart step," Mr. Alexander agrees. "Without you having an appointed guardian in place, the court would have appointed one for you. Your dad didn't know who they'd pick, so he wanted to get ahead of the game."

I hear him but I can't make myself answer him. I don't even look at him. All I can do is stare at the woman holding onto my arm.

Someone with something to gain.

GREY

$\mathcal{M}$y fingers are shaky when I dial Lilah's cell phone number. I hated giving her a cell phone, even though she was getting involved in more and more extracurricular activities as she grew older, but I didn't feel like I had much of a choice. More than anything in the world, I needed to make sure that my daughter was going to be safe.

At the time, the cell phone had been pretty much the only thing that I needed to do that. Now, though, in order to keep my own daughter safe, I actually had to sign a paper to give someone else guardianship rights over her.

I can only imagine what Sara would say.

Then again, if she were still alive, none of this would be happening. She would have been there the entire time, making sure that Lilah was safe, making sure that she wasn't falling apart without me.

Sara. Not Carol Matthews.

As tightly as I grip the receiver while I listen to the phone ring, frustration and pain grip my heart even more. All of my life I've done everything I can to help and save people, and the thought that anyone could believe that I'd actually hurt someone on purpose is enough to make me sick.

"Hello?" A kind voice on the other end of the line picks up. I know immediately that it isn't my daughter, but it still takes me a moment to realize who it is.

"Carol," I say, and relief courses through my body. All I want is for Lilah to be okay. The best thing for her right now is to have Carol taking care of her. I still feel guilty that I'm not the one with my daughter right now, but I will be soon enough. I just have to get through this and make them realize that I'm not guilty.

Even Jeremy Alexander says that the evidence they have against me is weak, circumstantial at best. They're grasping at straws, and why they've zeroed in on me as their main suspect I have no idea. It doesn't matter, I suppose. All that matters is getting home to Lilah.

"Grey. How are you? Are you holding up okay? Getting enough to eat?" Carol's voice is full of worry and I close my eyes for a moment, forcing myself to slow down and take a few deep breaths before I answer.

"I'm okay," I tell her, which isn't entirely true, but I'm not going to admit just how awful it is here while I wait for my fate to be decided. "How's Lilah? Is she okay?"

"She's fine. I took her cell phone away because I caught her reading the news on it again and I didn't want her to fill her head with all of that worry. The last thing that she needs right now is to be focused on what's happening to you instead of thinking about how she's going to make it through this."

I don't know that I agree with that line of thinking one hundred percent, but there's nothing that I can do from jail, and I don't really want to argue with the woman taking care of my daughter. "Thank you for agreeing to be her guardian," I say, and she answers with a low chuckle.

"Of course. It's the right thing for Lilah." There's a slight pause and I can tell that she wants to ask me something but is afraid to bring it up. "Did you see the paperwork giving me access to some of your accounts? I want to be able to pay your bills and make sure that Lilah has everything that she needs, but I unfortunately don't have enough money of my own to do that right now. The divorce is proving more expensive than I thought it would be..."

Of course. The divorce. Mentally, I smack my forehead, then feel even guiltier for asking her to take on full guardianship of Lilah. I never even thought about the fact that her finances might be tight.

"I haven't seen it yet, no, but I'll call Mr. Alexander first thing in the morning," I promise her. "I want you to be able to have whatever you need to take care of Lilah."

She sounds relieved. "Thank you, Grey. I feel terrible asking for something like that, but without a little help, I don't know how in the world I'd be able to pay for everything myself."

"Don't feel terrible. Seriously. I should have thought of it myself. I apologize." I run my hand through my hair and look around. Nobody's watching me, but I can see a guard sitting close enough to jump up and intervene if I do something that I shouldn't.

That's one of the most unnerving things about being in here: there's always someone right there. Always someone listening, watching, waiting. No matter what I'm doing, I don't have any privacy.

"Well, I know that you didn't call to talk to me," Carol says, "and Lilah looks like she's going to come out of her skin if I don't give her phone, so here you go."

"Thank you," I say. There's a shuffling sound, then I hear my daughter on the phone.

"Dad? Are you okay?" Her voice is soft and sad, the words spilling out of her like she can't quite hold them back and I blink hard, closing my eyes against the burning sensation. Tears are threatening to spill out and my chest feels tight, even though I swore to myself that I wasn't going to cry.

"Lilah, I'm doing all right. How are you? Are you eating? Sleeping? Feeling okay?" I want nothing more than to see her and hug her. With my eyes closed, I can see what she looks like, but not being able to actually touch her is enough to make me feel like I'm going crazy.

"I'm terrible," she admits, and I take a pained breath in.

Of course she is. How could she be anything but awful with me sitting behind bars and her wondering every moment of every day what's going to happen to me?

"I know, Lilah," I say. "I'm sorry. I'm doing everything I can to get home as quickly as possible."

"About that." She pauses and I hear movement, like she's pacing. "I think that I found some evidence that I need to get to the police."

My heart leaps even though I know that the chances that she found something on her own that will really help me are slim to none. If the professional detectives missed it, how in the world is a young girl like Lilah supposed to come up with some evidence that could help me? I want to believe that she found something, but I'm afraid to.

"Lilah, don't get your hopes up," I warn, wanting to temper her expectations.

"They're already up, Dad." A pause and I wonder what she's doing. When she speaks again, her voice is such a low whisper that I have to strain my ears to hear. "I think that Mrs. Matthews is the killer."

My heart sinks. Any of the hope that I felt that Lilah could have actually found something meaningful that could help me flies right out the window. I reach out, grabbing onto the wall to support me. I feel like my legs could give way at any moment and I would just sink to the floor, unable to get back up again, beaten and defeated.

"Lilah," I say, and I can hear the pain in my voice. I don't know if she can as well, I hope not, but it doesn't matter. She has to listen to me, whether she wants to or not. "Lilah, you're panicking," I tell her. "You're grasping at straws and trying to make connections where there aren't any. Please, don't do this. Don't become suspicious of the one person who's trying to help us right now."

"But, Dad," she hisses, her voice low. "You don't understand what I saw in her car! She's the killer, I know that she is!"

"Lilah!" My voice is so loud that it not only surprises me, but causes the guard to look over at me. I give him an apologetic smile and lower my voice to a more acceptable level. "Lilah, honey, don't do this. Drop it. Whatever is going through your head right now, you need to get it out. I'm serious."

"So am I. She took my laptop battery, too, Dad. What do you think about that?" Anger coats her every word, snaking tightly around my head and squeezing. My head hurts just talking to my daughter, which isn't something that I'm used to, nor like.

"Lilah, stop. You need to get some rest and I bet that you'll feel a lot better in the morning, okay? Trust me, Carol Matthews is looking out for you and wouldn't do anything to try to hurt you. You have to let her help you. Please."

Silence. I know that a lot of dads talk about getting the silent treatment from their kids, but I've never experienced it before. I shift, waiting for her to break it but already knowing that she's not going to.

"I have to go," I finally say. "I'll call you again as soon as I can, Lilah, but seriously, I want you to drop it. I don't know what you've got going on in your head right now, but it's not helpful. I love you."

"I love you." Her voice is flat. "Bye, Dad."

She hangs up before I can get a chance to say anything else and I gently put the receiver back down on its cradle. I want to take it and smash it into the wall but there's no way that that would end up well.

"All done?" the guard asks, and when I nod despondently, he gestures back to my cell.

I walk in front of him, thinking. Even though I don't want to give any credence to what Lilah said, I can't get her words out of my head.

There's just no way that Carol Matthews is the killer.

CAROL

"Get up, darling," I say, flipping on Lilah's light and strolling into her room. She cried herself to sleep last night and I had to listen to it echoing down the hall. If anyone should be tired, it should be me, but no. I was up early to make coffee and start figuring out how to pay bills.

Not that I expect her to thank me. When I think about it, Lilah has been nothing but ungrateful since I moved in here to take care of her. After talking to her dad yesterday she was downright rude to me. I'm really going to have to rethink letting her talk to him again anytime soon.

If she's going to have a terrible attitude after she gets off the phone with him then there's just no reason for her to talk to him. That's how I see it, anyway, and I can't imagine that Grey would argue with me if he really stopped and thought things through.

Lilah still hasn't moved, so I grab the curtains and yank them open before pulling back the quilt mounded up over her body. "Lilah, time to get up," I say firmly. "We're going to the bank this morning so that I can get some money, and then we're going to the grocery store. It's time that all of the junk in the house gets thrown out."

"We don't have junk in the house," she argues, rolling over to glare at me. She sits up, staring at me like she wants to make me disappear. "Dad doesn't buy junk."

I glare back. "I saw the candy stash in the back of the freezer. It's gone. Get dressed and come downstairs to get something to eat, quick smart, we have a very busy day ahead of us." I turn from her, but not before noticing how rough she looks. If that's what she looks like every single morning then I'm going to have to ask her to put on makeup and get properly dressed before coming downstairs.

She looks a fright, that's for certain. I believe that everyone should take steps to make themselves look nice before they interact with other people. I never let George see me in the morning before I'd fixed my hair and my makeup and I'm sure that he appreciated it.

As I walk down the hall, I glance in the guest room where I've been staying. Making coffee wasn't the only thing that I did this morning. I was up early enough to wash the sheets on both that bed and the one in the master bedroom and put them back on. Now the guest room is all ready for someone to come stay here.

I moved all my things into the master bedroom. I'm in charge of the house now and it makes sense that I'd have my things in the largest room. I can't wait to sleep in there tonight. It's the kind of bedroom that I always dreamed of when I was growing up, but never got to have.

There's a huge four-poster bed, and double doors leading out to a second-floor balcony directly across from the bed. Even though it's summer and hot out, I fully intend to sleep with those doors open tonight. If I get warm and the breeze isn't enough to cool me off then I'll just crank up the AC.

From what I've seen on the bank statements, Grey has more than enough money for me to stay comfortable in here, even if I do run the AC and keep the windows open at the same time. He's been stashing it away for years and could probably retire if he was smart with his money. Some people get more than they deserve.

He's definitely one of those people. After taking George from me, he deserved to lose everything, but he's somehow managed to make a wonderful life for himself while I was struggling so much. It's time that he gets what's coming to him and I finally get to be happy again.

Downstairs I pour myself another cup of coffee and take a sip, closing my eyes to really taste the flavor. It's exceptional. This isn't pre-ground grocery store coffee. I'd never even heard of the brand before, but when I looked it up online, I saw that you can only order it direct from a small group of farmers in Guatemala.

As I wait for Lilah to join me, I run down the list of things I want to get done today. The bank is first, of course, then straight to the grocery store to make sure that we have good food in the house. It's going to be impossible for Lilah to lose her attitude if she's sneaking candy and giving herself sugar crashes all the time. After that, I have some bills to pay to keep the lights and water on in here, and need to talk to Mr. Taylor to make sure that everything is moving forward with my divorce.

It's such an exciting time in my life right now and I feel more than a little giddy. For the first time in years, since George died, I feel like I have things under control. I honestly feel like things might actually work out the way that I deserve. This is the type of house I should have lived in my entire life. I should have always had amazing coffee like this.

Now that this is my life, I'm not going to take it for granted. I have a lot of boring things to do this morning, but there are also some other errands to run later this afternoon that will be a little more fun. If I'm going to live here and be Lilah's guardian, then I need to look the part. There's nothing wrong with my clothes and hair, but they make me look like I'm a math teacher, not like I'm independently wealthy.

I bet that taking Lilah shopping would help make her feel warmer towards me. All girls love to shop, so I'll take her to the mall and offer to get us new hairstyles as well. Maybe a pedicure, too, to help win her over.

In time she'll figure out that I'm the best thing to ever happen to her. Her father simply can't provide for her the way that I can. Sure, he's the one who made the money, but I'm going to spend it in ways that will actually help her out. I'm tired of not getting what I deserve from life, and Lilah is going to get to enjoy all of the results of my hard work right alongside me. If I get a pedicure, she can get one too.

I'm about to go back upstairs to look for her again when she finally comes down, looking more exhausted than ever. She slips into the kitchen without a word and sits at the counter, resting her head in her hands.

I stare at her. Her hair is unkempt and her eyes are bloodshot. Even though it's not warm in the house, she still has a sheen of sweat glistening on her forehead. "Are you sick?" I ask after a moment of looking at her.

"I don't feel so good." She wraps her arms around her waist and gives a little moan.

Is she faking? I walk around the counter to get a better look at her but I don't want to get too close to her in case she's contagious. That was always the worst part of teaching. Knowing that you were locked in a room with germy kids and that you couldn't get out into the fresh air made me feel sick most every day I was at work. I can't even fathom how many times I washed my hands on a daily basis just to keep from coming down with something.

I could reach out and feel her forehead to see if she's warm, but I'd rather not touch her. "Do you have a thermometer?" I ask, and I'm not surprised when she gives me a half-hearted shrug.

"Dad kept it somewhere," she says, "but I don't know where. He'd just bring it out for me when I didn't feel good and then put it away when he was done with it."

"What a good father," I say automatically, without really thinking. "Maybe if you eat something you'll feel better." I move to the kitchen to make her some toast or eggs, but as soon as my back is to her, she starts to gag. The sound is enough to make me come out of my skin and I stare at her, backing up. "Go to bed," I tell her, pointing.

If she gets sick in the kitchen then I swear I might get sick as well. There are few things worse than someone throwing up. You always have to help clean them up and I can't stand the thought. To be honest, I wasn't entirely sure that I wanted her to come with me on my morning errands anyway. Now I'm positive I don't. I'm sure that she'd just stink up the car.

And I'm not taking my old beater, oh no. I have my eye on the black Range Rover in the garage. All things considered, if I'm going to enjoy this first day of the life that I've always deserved, then maybe it's best if Lilah stays behind. She'd just put a damper on it all.

LILAH

I watch from my bedroom window in disbelief as Mrs. Matthews backs my dad's Range Rover out of the garage. Leaning forward so that I can get a better view, I dig my fingernails into the windowsill and press my forehead up against the glass. It's nice and cool and should be making me feel better right now, but it's not.

I wasn't lying about not feeling great. Okay, I wasn't really about to throw up in the kitchen, but I had a pretty good feeling that if Mrs. Matthews thought that I was that she'd leave me behind when she went out, and I was right. Fine. I don't want to be with her any more than she wants to be with me.

My stomach churns and I step away from the window, trying to think about what I can do. She took away my phone, my laptop is dead, and I don't know how in the world I'm going to prove that she was the murderer.

Then it hits me. I'm angry about her taking my dad's car, but that means that she left hers in the driveway. I rush back to the window and look down at it. It really is a piece of junk, but it may still have the evidence inside it that will free my dad from jail.

Yanking off my pajamas, I quickly pull on some clothes and then splash water on my face in the bathroom before taking two pain pills, hoping they kick in soon. The pounding in my head has to go away if I'm going to be able to think straight.

Even though I want to run down the stairs, I take them carefully. My body feels weak and I'm a little unsteady on my feet, so I don't want to accidentally fall. The fresh air from outside fills my lungs and helps to clear my head, and I look down the road in case she's coming back before trying the handle on her car.

It's locked.

Cupping my hand around my eyes, I press up against the glass and look inside. I know that I'm not going to be able to see the notebook from here, but my eyes still go straight to the center console. It's closed tightly and nothing looks out of place in the vehicle.

I walk around the car, trying each of the doors in turn. None of them budge, not even the trunk. Turning around in a circle, I look for anyone who is around who might be able to help me break in.

Break in. That's it. In a rush of excitement, I hurry over to the garden and grab a rock from the border. I remember when my mom chose these to decorate her garden beds. They're all smooth and just a bit bigger than I can comfortably hold in one hand.

My head pounds as I pick it up, using both hands to carry it back to the car. I still feel weak and a little wobbly but I'm not going to stop now. Standing back a few feet from the car, I heave the rock and throw it as hard as I can, aiming it right at the driver's window.

The rock hits the glass with a loud cracking sound, but it doesn't shatter the window completely. The rock falls to the driveway with a loud clatter.

On a good day it wouldn't be heavy at all, but I don't feel good right now and I groan as I walk over to the rock. It honestly takes all of my energy to pick it up and prepare to throw it again.

This time when it hits the glass the loud crunching sound of the glass breaking fills the air even more and spiderweb cracks shoot out from the impact, reaching out to the edges of the window. The rock still doesn't break through but I have a pretty good feeling that I'm almost there. Just one more good hit and I'll be in the car.

As long as the notebook is still in there, I'm okay. Then I can save my dad.

The rock is right by the car. "You got this, Lilah," I say to myself, trying to psych myself up. I'm so close. Walking over to the rock, I pick it back up from the ground, lifting it up to my hip where I rest it for a moment.

This time, a grunt leaves my mouth when I throw the rock. I put everything that I have into it and almost lose my balance when the rock leaves my hands. It sails right at the window and makes a direct hit, lodging itself halfway through the glass. Nervously, I glance around in case a neighbor is watching, but all of the houses are still.

Most people are probably already at work, and any wives left behind have probably started self-medicating by now. Nobody would look out the window at me, and even if they did, I don't know if they'd call the police. Instead, they'd probably just watch.

When I open the door bits of broken glass fall to the driveway like glittering jewels. The driver's seat is covered in glass, so I hit the button to unlock the doors and scoot around the car, slipping in on the passenger's side. Taking a deep breath, I open the center console.

The notebook is gone.

"No," I whisper, digging frantically through the console. Her winter gloves are still there, as is the pen that she probably used to write in the notebook, but the notebook itself is missing. Slamming the lid shut, I open the glove box right in front of me, pawing through it and pulling everything out so that I can really look for the notebook.

Nothing.

It's not under the seats, nor tucked into the visor. Slumping back in my seat, I wipe my forehead with the back of my hand and try to think. She must have moved it after leaving me alone in the car yesterday. I'm sure that she realized that that was a terrible idea and hid it somewhere else. Like in her luggage?

I get out of the car and hurry to the house as quickly as I can go. My legs are heavy, like they're weighted with lead, but I still force myself to move as fast as possible. Once inside, I slam and lock the front door, then make my way upstairs to the guest room.

I step in the room, not believing what I'm seeing. It's immaculate, the bed is made, nothing is out of place, and all her belongings are gone. Dropping to my knees, I look under the bed, like I expect to see her luggage, but it's not there, nor is it in the closet.

Did she actually move into my dad's bedroom? The one he shared with Mom? I stumble out the door and down the hall, throwing open the door to look. This room looks perfectly put together too, but I notice immediately all of the details that are wrong. I see her phone charger plugged in by the bed, her nightgown folded on the pillow.

Her luggage is under the bed and she's moved her hairbrush and perfume onto my dad's dresser, which has been cleared of all of his pictures and knick-knacks, tucked away God knows where.

Now I'm really going to throw up. Rushing to the bathroom, I hunch over the toilet and empty my stomach. Cramps shoot through my body and a cold sweat breaks out on my chest and forehead. I finally stand up, grabbing the cup from the sink to rinse the taste of vomit out of my mouth. It's right by her makeup and I sweep it all off of the counter, screaming.

Rage courses through me even though I know that I need to do my best to control it. Grabbing the counter, I stare in the mirror at myself, panting. "You have to find it," I say, giving myself a little nod. "You don't have a choice."

My body screams at me to go to bed, but I don't listen to it. I spin out of the bathroom and fall to my knees at the edge of the bed, yanking all of her luggage out as quickly as possible. It's in here. I know that it is. It's got to be.

I'm going to find it and then I'm going to get my dad back.

CAROL

*T*o be honest, being on my own to run errands is much more pleasant than having Lilah with me. At first, I thought that she was a lovely girl, if perhaps a touch out of control, but the more time that I spend with her, the more I realize that she needs some serious professional help.

She'll need therapy once her dad goes to prison for murder, and I'm more than happy to use his money to pay for it. Boarding school also seems like a great option for her. It would ensure that she gets a good education and, frankly, would give me a lot more time to do the things that I love.

Well...maybe it won't be the absolute *best* education. I don't know that I want to spend the money on that, because let's face it, she's not that bright. It just needs to be good enough for her to be a productive member of society. Goodness, how things have changed since the beginning, when I thought that I wanted to take on the role of her mother figure.

Not anymore. With the way she's been acting recently, I

just want her gone. If she could be the least bit grateful then I'd want her to stay in her house, of course I would—I'm not a monster. Right now, though, she's acting out. She's ungrateful, snotty, and rude. It's a shame. We could have a lot of fun together if only she would get her attitude in check.

I load the groceries into the back of the Range Rover. I'd love to go straight to the mall to go shopping, but I probably need to get everything home so that it gets into the fridge before I head back out. It's inconvenient, but nobody will ever be able to say that I didn't do things for other people.

As I drive back home, I turn on the radio and sing along. The leather seats are so soft and the Range Rover handles so well that I know that I've made the correct decision. Even though I've never doubted it, not since I came up with the plan, it's times like these that underline that I'm doing the right thing.

I deserve to be happy and comfortable, especially after all that's happened to me in my life. So many people get taken advantage of and screwed over every single day, and most of them aren't willing to stand up for themselves and do what they can do put a stop to it. I am.

That's how I'm different. That's how I know that I'm going to survive.

My pulse quickens as I pull up into the driveway. The glass on the driver's side window of my car is broken out. The doors are all shut, and I know immediately that this isn't the work of some neighborhood hoodlum.

It was Lilah.

It had to be her. Fear grips my heart when I think about the possibility that she saw my notebook in the center console yesterday when I left her in the car. It was a stupid mistake on my part, but I've had her in the car with me many times before and never worried about her poking around where she wasn't allowed.

I have a sudden urge to tear into the house immediately and hunt through it for Lilah, but instead I pull into the garage and sit for a moment with the door closed, thinking.

If she found the notebook in the car then she's probably looking for it right now. I don't think that she'll ever find it, but I can see her now, tearing my room apart as she tries to find it. That's not good, but I have her phone and I dismantled her computer.

There's literally no way that she could possibly contact the police, even if she found anything. Or was even just suspicious.

"Okay, Lilah, let's see what you've been up to," I say to myself, getting out of the car. I was so worried just a few minutes ago about the food in the trunk spoiling while I shopped, but right now I don't care if it all goes bad.

I can go shopping again, but first I need to make sure that Lilah didn't find anything that she's not supposed to.

"Lilah...darling...?" I call, stepping into the kitchen from the garage. It's deadly silent on the ground floor of the house but I take a quick tour through it anyway, wanting to make sure that I don't somehow miss her. She's not in the living room reading, nor in her dad's study. I pause in the door of that room.

How many times I have mentally rearranged it so that it will be my study and not Grey Bennett's? Now his daughter is threatening to ruin everything, the little minx.

I take the stairs two at a time, moving even faster when I hear a thud coming from my bedroom. Almost running now, I round the corner into the room, my eyes darting around as I look for her.

She's crouched next to the bed, rummaging through all

of my luggage. She's pulled it all out from under the bed and is sitting in the middle of it all, her face pale and sweaty, her eyes wide. When she hears me in the doorway she pauses and looks up at me, her mouth set in a firm line.

"What did you do to them?" She asks, staggering to her feet. Something's definitely really wrong with her. She didn't look so great when I left the house earlier, but it's obvious now that she feels even worse. Lilah wipes her hand across her forehead as she stares at me and waits for an answer.

"To whom?" I ask sweetly, walking into the room, slowly moving closer to her. She's really sick, I can see that right away. If she feels as bad as she looks, feverish possibly verging on delirious, then she won't be able to think or move quickly. Is it entirely possible that, once she sleeps and wakes up, she'll think that this was all a bad dream?

As much as I'd like to believe that, I know it's not true.

It's too late. Something has to happen to Lilah. I thought that just sending her to boarding school after her dad's trial would be more than enough for me, but maybe that's too good for her. I realize with a start that I don't want to ever see her again. I want Lilah gone, but I'm not sure how I can manage that and keep control of the house and the finances.

"Those men. My dad's patients." She wipes some hair away from her forehead and stares at me, reaching out to rest her hand on the bed for balance. "I know that you killed them and framed my dad. Why? Why would you do that?"

"You don't look so good," I say soothingly, reaching for her. "Come here and let me help you into bed, dear." I reach for her, fully expecting her to soften and let me lead her down the hall. It would be so tempting to push her down the stairs as we pass them, but I have to refrain from doing something that rash.

Instead of letting me take her arm, though, she lashes out at me, yanking her arm away to keep me from being able to grab her. "Don't touch me," she hisses. "I know what you are. You're just trying to tear my family apart. Well, you succeeded. Congratulations. I don't know why, yet, but I know that you're not the angel we thought that we needed so badly."

"You're sick," I tell her. I want to hurt her. God, I want to punish Lilah for what she's saying to me, but I know better than to do that. As good as it would feel, I'd lose everything that I worked so hard for. Even though I'd make it look like an accident, if there was no Lilah needing a guardian, there wouldn't be any reason for me to live in the house any longer. I'd have to go back to Trent, have to try to get him to take me back.

I simply won't allow that to happen.

"I'm not sick," she snaps. "You're a murderer, Honey. You're a monster."

That's enough. I've been called a lot of things in my life, and not all of them were kind, but I draw the line at monster. "Shut up," I hiss at her, moving faster than her, not pulling her in for a hug this time but making sure that she can't slip away from me.

"Stop it!" She cries, struggling against my grip. Unfortunately for Lilah, though, today she is too weak. She simply doesn't have the energy to fight me as I pull her down the hall with me. As I take her to her room, my mind races with all the things I need to do.

I have to get rid of her—for now.

I have to clean up the glass outside so that a nosy neighbor doesn't notice and decide to get involved.

And I have to get the fool groceries in from the car. I picked up some gorgeous truffles and chanterelles for myself to celebrate all of my hard work finally paying off, and there's no way that I'm going to let Lilah ruin it for me.

LILAH

*M*rs. Matthews pushes me roughly through the door into my bedroom and I almost lose my balance. Even though I'm shaky on my feet, I turn around as quickly as possible to try to get back out into the hall. I know that notebook is in the house somewhere. I have to find it, have to find proof that she's the one who murdered those four men.

Then I have to get the proof to the police somehow.

"Let me out!" I cry, reaching for the door. Mrs. Matthews leers at me, her face dark with rage, and slams the door shut. I hear the click of the handle as it slips into place and I grab it, doing my best to turn it, then I hear the bolt slide across.

She's locked me in.

When we first moved into this house when I was a little girl I'd been amazed at all of the locks on the outside of the bedrooms. They're up top near the ceiling, much higher than I could reach at the time, and I remember the discussion that my mom and dad had one night about taking them off the door. My mom wanted to take them off because she didn't want anyone to think that our family would lock someone in their room.

My dad had laughed and tousled my hair, telling her that nobody would think that about our family. He thought that the locks added some interest to the old house. Eventually, the vote came down to me. At first, I'd wanted to side with my mom because she and I agreed on everything, but I had to admit that I thought the bolts were pretty cool and made me think of a castle, which of course made me a princess.

"Promise me that you won't ever lock me in," I'd said, crossing my arms on my chest and pouting. Mom and Dad had both laughed and agreed, and that was it.

The locks stayed.

Now I wish more than anything that we had removed them. Reaching up, I grab the doorknob and give it a twist, knowing it's futile even as I try. "Please," I call as loudly as I can. "I'm sorry! Please, Mrs. Matthews."

It's hopeless and I know that. Even if she could hear me, which I honestly don't think that she can, there's no way that she'd ever let me back out of my room right now. I'm being punished and the only thing that there is for me to do is just to wait it out and see what happens next.

Panic overtakes me and I slam myself up against the door again, trying to get out. It shakes and I think that I hear the wood splintering, but maybe I'm just imagining it because the door doesn't move. Leaning my head against the wood and slipping to the ground, I swear in frustration.

I don't think that she will actually hurt me, or worse. If she's been working this hard this whole time to move into the house and take over, then she has to keep me alive, or she will only ruin her chances of getting what she wants.

That thought doesn't make me feel much better, but somehow I manage to push myself up to my hands and knees and crawl over to my bed. My head is throbbing so badly that every little movement sends shivers of pain down my spine. I have no idea how I got so sick or what I picked up, but I'm willing to bet that I need to see a doctor.

I'm also willing to bet that there's no way that Mrs. Matthews is going to take me to one right now. I showed my hand when I accused her of being a murderer, and now even though I have no proof she has every reason to keep me locked up in the house.

"Stupid," I mutter, pulling myself up on the bed. The window is right there and I stumble over to it, leaning against the glass to look down at the driveway. Whatever she's doing, she hasn't cleaned up the glass yet. It's still glittering on the driveway like someone dropped diamonds out there. Why a neighbor hasn't looked out their window and called the police yet, I don't know, but I need their help. Without a phone or laptop, I'm totally on my own.

My fingers are almost too tired and crampy to work, but I manage to unlatch the window. It takes all of my body weight under the window and pushing up hard with my shoulder to make it slide up in its tracks.

How many times since my mom died have I opened this window and snuck out to read on the roof? I'm sure that my dad knows that I'm doing it, but he's never tried to stop me even though the roof slants dangerously out from under my window. I hesitate, wondering if I have the necessary balance to shimmy down the slanted part of the roof and scoot over to the flatter section. I've done it dozens of times with a book tucked under my arm, but never when I was this sick. And once I get out there, then what?

. . .

I can only imagine myself trying to jump down from the roof to the ground. Maybe on a good day I'd be able to stick the landing, but there's a voice in the back of my head telling me that I'm setting myself up for a broken leg if I try anything this stupid in my current condition.

"Come on, Lilah," I mutter to myself. "You've really got to do better than breaking both of your legs on the front lawn right now." I stay by the window, though, and I suck in a breath when I see Mrs. Matthews leaving the garage. She has a broom and a dustpan and walks straight to her car to clean up the glass.

Never once does she even look around to see if anyone is watching. The way she moves exudes confidence, almost like she's daring someone to try to stop her from doing what needs to be done.

I don't want her to see me watching her and I pull back from the window. I need to figure something out. Turning, I look around my room. My eyes fall on my dead laptop, but I shake my head.

"If only there was a way to turn that on," I say to myself, then it hits me. Just because my laptop doesn't turn on doesn't mean that I don't have something that will. My dad has always been really good about upgrading my phone each year, but instead of throwing out the old ones, I've always hung onto them.

Just in case one breaks. Just in case I have a friend who needs one. Just in case I've been locked in my room by a crazy lady who's also a murderess.

I can't believe I didn't think of it before. Dropping to my knees, I pull a shoe box out from under my bed and flip open the lid. Sitting in it are three cell phones, all of them wiped clean of my info, all of them dead. Under the phones is a snarl of chargers, and I grab one, fitting it into a phone, then turn and crawl across the floor to an outlet.

GREY

J got the call that Jeremy was here to see me right after lunch. Even though we didn't have a meeting scheduled, there wasn't any way that I was going to tell my lawyer that I didn't want to see him. And it wasn't like I had anything else to do.

My hands are handcuffed in front of me, the metal cool on my wrists as I walk down the hall to my meeting room. One thing that nobody tells you about jail is how mind-numbingly boring it is. It doesn't matter what I want to do, or how much energy I have, by the time lunch is over, all I want to do is sleep.

Part of me wondered for a while if there was something in the food designed to make inmates feel a bit sleepy. It certainly would cut down on fights and problems, but I know that's not true. The truth is it probably a lot less sinister and much simpler.

When you eat and have no way to work it off, you just want to sleep.

"He's in there," my guard says, pointing to the door we're standing in front of, like I couldn't possibly have figured it out on my own. Even though I feel a short reply come to my lips, I bite it back and give him a smile and a nod.

"Thank you," I tell him, enjoying the way surprise flits across his face. Nobody in here is polite, I've noticed that.

"Grey." Jeremy's standing when I walk into the small room, a look of triumph on his face. It's not one that I've seen him wear before and I almost feel myself getting hopeful, but I push that thought way, way down.

Until I know for sure what's going on, there's no way that I'm going to allow myself to feel anything remotely like happiness. I'm here, in jail, and so far it looks like the case against me is weak but holding. Jeremy's words, not mine.

"To what do I owe this pleasure?" I ask. My legs are tired and I want to sit down, but he's still standing, so I don't make a move to the table yet. My eyes are locked on his as I wait for him to answer. "Jeremy? What's going on? Why are you here?"

I've done everything asked of me. I made sure that Lilah would be safe by asking Carol to take care of her. I made sure that she had access to my accounts so she could pay any bills and make sure that Lilah was taken care of.

I've cooperated with the detectives, right from the beginning. I've kept my cool and done everything that they wanted me to do.

Never once have I seen Jeremy look this happy about anything.

"They're dropping all charges," he says, and just like that my legs give out. I sway, grabbing the chair back in front of me. Even though I heard what he said, I still can't believe it. "What?" I manage. My voice sounds like a frog, but I don't bother clearing my throat to try again. He heard me the first time. He gives me a little nod of confirmation.

"They're dropping all charges," he repeats, and I close my eyes to let the words wash over me. They feel like baptism water, like they're going to absolve me of all of my sins and finally help me get my life back. I want to hear him saying them over and over, but first I have to know what happened.

"What...?" I ask, then stop, unable to finish the question. My throat is tight and dry and I swallow hard, letting go of the chair so that I can stand up and look at him.

"You're going to want to sit down," he tells me with a smile, gesturing at the chair.

I glance at it but don't move. When Jeremy takes the seat across from me I finally sit, but I'm perched on the edge of it, unable to look away from him. All I care about right now is him telling me what happened and then me getting to go see my daughter. She must be elated and I wonder if she knows what happened.

"Talk to me," I say.

"It was Lilah," he says, giving me a smile. "She figured it all out on her own and called the police using an old cell phone."

I frown, not following. "An old cell phone? What are you talking about? Start over, Jeremy, I have no idea what you're saying. For a start, how could she call anyone on an old cell phone if it doesn't have a plan?" My head is spinning.

"Okay, here goes." He exhales hard, planting his hands on the table between us like he needs something that will keep him grounded. "I don't know if you realize it, Grey, but Lilah's been trying to find out who really killed your patients. When she did, she was able to call out using an old cell phone. Even when they don't have service, most still able to call 911, so that's what she did."

I exhale hard, sitting back in my chair. My head is still spinning with questions that I want to ask him. "Is Lilah okay?"

Jeremy nods. "She has a bad flu and is at the hospital to make sure that she doesn't need fluids, but there's an officer with her to make sure that she's safe. No worries about Lilah." He looks so pleased with himself that I feel myself start to smile in return.

I'm glad that my daughter is okay, but Jeremy still hasn't told me everything. "And the murderer? They've caught him? Who was it?"

Jeremy grins at me. "You're never going to believe it. It was Carol Matthews."

My chest squeezes tight and my jaw drops open as I look at my friend. "Carol Matthews?" I repeat, unsure that I heard him correctly. "You can't be serious. She's been watching Lilah. She's...she's her guardian right now." I feel like I'm going to be sick.

Before I can ask any other questions, the door opens and an officer stands in it, framed by the light from the hall. "Dr. Bennett, if you'd like to come with me, you're free to go. The DA's office has filed all of the paperwork to let you out of here."

I turn from looking at him to Jeremy. I know I should move, but I feel frozen in place, like I can't quite get my body to respond to what I want it to do.

"Go," Jeremy tells me. "I'll wait for you and take you to see Lilah."

As I stand up and follow the officer out the door I fully expect to wake up from a dream. There's no way that this is actually happening. Each step feels like it takes forever as I follow him down to the processing room. There, he takes off my cuffs and I rub my wrists while he speaks.

"You're free to go, Dr. Bennett," he tells me. "Of course, there will be some more paperwork to fill out, but from what we understand, your daughter is in the hospital. I'm sure you want to get to her."

"Thank you," I manage, then clear my throat to try again. "Thanks. So...I can just...go?"

Ahead of me is the door leading outside. It seems so surreal that I would just be allowed to walk out of it, but that's apparently what's happening. While I wait for the man to answer, I look at his name tag. *Corn.*

"Yep. You're free, Dr. Bennett. The DA will be calling you, I'm sure, to talk about what happened, but right now there's nothing that you need to do." He hands me a bag with the clothing that I was wearing when I was arrested.

I heft it, thinking about changing, but I really just want to get to Lilah.

Through the window I see Jeremy waiting by the car. Taking a deep breath, I walk past the officer and push open the door.

LILAH

I don't know exactly where I am but I do know that I feel like utter dirt. Hammered dirt. A bag of hammered dirt, set on fire, and then left on someone's front porch, if you get my drift. My entire body aches and it's hard for me to think straight.

There's an annoying beeping coming from somewhere near my head and I turn to look at it, but the bright lights overhead me make me close my eyes again as quickly as possible. When I swallow it feels like I'm trying to swallow a handful of rocks and dirt. Everything hurts and I wish that I could just fall asleep, but that's as impossible as getting comfortable.

"Lilah?"

A man's voice cuts through my thoughts and tugs at my mind through the pain. It sounds just like my dad, which is about as cruel as it can be. I know that he's not here, he's in jail, and I close my eyes, hot tears squeezing from the corners before they run down my cheeks.

I feel hot, like I've been in the desert all day long, and I shift, turning my head away from the voice.

Someone touches my cheek. "Lilah." It's the same voice, only this time it's not a question. I suck in a deep breath and marvel at how unfair this is. Whoever is touching me right now sounds so much like my dad that I don't think I can handle it.

"Can she hear me?" It's the same voice. I can't make out the response, but I do hear someone murmur an answer. For a moment, the room is silent except for the beeping, then the voice tries again.

"Lilah, it's your dad. Can you look at me?"

A shiver runs through me. I'm going to open my eyes and look at this person just so I can prove to myself that it isn't my dad. Rolling my head to the side, I slowly force my eyes open.

At first, the figure standing over me is blurry and I can't seem to bring them into focus. I blink a few times, then lift my hand to rub my eyes. There's an IV in the back of my hand and it pulls when I move. The man leans closer, blocking out the bright light that's hurting my eyes so badly.

And I see that it's my dad.

"Dad!" I want to scream out his name, I'm so excited, but all that comes out of me is a soft whisper. "Dad! Is that you?"

I could be so sick that I'm hallucinating. That's entirely possible, but I push the thought from my mind. Even if I am so ill that I'm seeing things, I want nothing more than for my dad to be standing over me. I can handle this being a dream as long as it takes away some of the pain that I feel right now.

"Lilah, it's me." He falls to his knees next to my bed, grabbing my hands in his.

I blink against the lights and he must notice because he turns and speaks to the person standing in the door. "Turn them off, please," he says, and immediately the room is bathed not in the bright light but in a soft glow that's warm and comforting.

"How are you here? Is this real?" I squeeze his hands. They're so warm and soft that I know that it must be him, but I still can't believe that it's true. "How did you get out?"

"You," he tells me. "You got me out." In a smooth motion, he moves to sit on the edge of my bed. "Even sick as a puppy, you somehow managed to figure it all out and call the cops. What in the world goes on inside this amazing head of yours, Lilah?"

I shake my head a little, but it makes my head feel like it's splitting in two. That's not something I want to do again. "It's just the flu," I manage. "I don't know where I picked it up, but before it got too bad I was able to put it all together. It was Mrs. Matthews, dad. She killed them all."

"You don't have the flu," he says, his voice sad. "I spoke to the doctor and it turns out that she's been giving you something to make you sick. It wouldn't have been enough to kill you, but it was obvious that she wanted you out of commission, so she put something in your water."

"My water?" I can't even remember when I drank something that she might have compromised. "When?"

"The glass on your desk, Lilah. The doctor said that you'll be in the hospital at least overnight but then you'll be just fine. How do you feel?"

How do I feel? Honestly?

My heart is working overtime, like it's trying to pump sludge through my veins. I have a splitting headache. Even the thought of moving my arms or legs is enough to make me want to cry. I don't know that I've ever felt this sick in my life, but it doesn't really matter, because my dad is home.

He's not the murderer, never was, and now everyone knows it.

"I'm okay," I tell him, which is half the truth and half a lie. "What did the police say? How did they put it all together?" I honestly don't remember anything after remembering about my old cell phones.

This makes him grin. "Try and relax, Lilah, because you're never going to believe how this all shook out."

My dad has always loved telling stories, and I have a pretty good feeling that this is going to be a great one. Even though I still don't feel good, I let myself sink down into the bed so that I'll be comfortable. "Go for it," I say.

"After you called the police, they rushed right to the house. Carol—Mrs. Matthews—greeted them and told them that there wasn't anyone there who would have made the call. Unfortunately, even though you were so sick, you had been smart enough to stay on the line with them. They came into the house and found you locked in your bedroom."

It's coming back to me now. I remember opening the window and thinking about crawling out but being so afraid to get hurt. Nodding, I squeeze his fingers, pressing him to continue.

"She tried to come up with some story about you locking yourself in there, but it was obvious that you hadn't done it. The door was locked from the outside. When EMS came you were only half-conscious, but you managed to tell them your suspicions. Something about a list of names?"

I nod, but I don't have the energy to speak. Seeing that, my dad continues.

"Mrs. Matthews became agitated and when the officers asked for her ID, she refused to give it to them. They rifled through her purse for her ID and that's when they saw the notebook with a list of names." He grins at me like there's something even better to tell me and I wait patiently. "Along with two bottles."

"Bottles?"

"One was salvia extract, just what was used for the murders, and the other was something else. She wouldn't tell them what it was, and the lab doesn't really know what to test for, but I'm sure it was what she gave you to make you so sick. She was putting it in water, Lilah. When she gave people the water they didn't even question that it might be poisoned."

Relief floods through my body. I honestly can't believe what all has happened to me and my father, and the thought that it might really all be over is so overwhelming that I have to choke back tears. My dad sees it and lightly cups my cheek.

"You are so brave, Lilah," he tells me. "If it weren't for you, I'd still be in jail. Now, I'm going to sit right over there while you rest, and I promise you, I'm not leaving this room."

I don't want to rest. I want him to take me home and let me sleep in my own bed, but my eyelids are so heavy that I can't help but let them close.

GREY

*J*eremy is with me, his eyes locked on the man by the front door. Lieutenant Sumpter, Detective Laite's boss, is standing there, his arms crossed on his chest, his eyes flicking between me and Lilah.

I don't like the way he's looking at my daughter. After what we've been through together, I'm willing to do anything to keep her safe and she knows it. But I push that feeling down.

"Dr. Bennett, do you remember a George Harrel? He was a patient of yours a long time ago." Lieutenant Sumpter shifts his weight from one foot to the other while he waits for my response. He looks the picture of physical health, like he should be the poster child for whatever type of training officers have to go through before getting hired.

"George Harrel? Of course I remember him. Why do you ask?" Even though I know that I haven't done anything wrong, I still feel nervous. George was the first patient that I ever had who didn't make it. How he even got as high on the transplant list as he did, I'll never know. He was sick when he came to me, and I did my best for him.

My entire team did. We thought that we were out of the woods for a while, but then he took a sudden turn for the worse and we lost him, right there on the operating table. It was horrible, but there wasn't anything that we could do about it.

"His wife was named Caroline," Lieutenant Sumpter says, watching me carefully, and I feel a shiver run up my spine.

I knew that I had recognized her. "Oh, my God," I whisper, reaching over to squeeze Lilah's hand in mine. "Caroline Harrel is Carol Matthews."

The lieutenant nods and Lilah looks at me curiously. "Wait, she was married before?"

"She was married to my patient," I say, turning to look at her. "After he died, I never saw her again. I had no idea what happened to her. I thought that I recognized her when I first saw her that day outside the waffle place. I should have tried to figure it out and not just ignored the feeling."

"So what? Did she target you?" Lilah's voice is high. "Did she do all this on purpose?"

The lieutenant clears his throat. "That's exactly it, Lilah. She admitted that she wanted to punish your dad for taking her husband from her. She's sick in the head, thought that she could just move into your place and live there without any repercussions."

"Her one true love," Lilah gasps out. "She told me that her necklace was from her one true love. George must have given it to her while he was alive."

There's a hard lump in my stomach and I swallow, trying to chase it away. Nothing that I do seems to make me feel any better, so I look straight at the man standing by the door. "What does all this mean for us?" I glance at Jeremy while I speak. Even though I didn't think I was really going to need him here, the last thing that I wanted was to run into some problems without my lawyer at my side.

He's staring at the detective like he honestly can't wait to hear what the man has to say.

"It means that you'll have to be witnesses in the trial," Lieutenant Sumpter says. "It means that you're still going to be in the news, Dr. Bennett, and the George Harrel business will come up again, but at least there won't be reporters camped out outside your house. Hopefully it means that in a little while you and Lilah are able to have a normal life again."

I don't know how normal of a life we'll ever be able to have, to be honest. I've been on the news far too much, my face plastered all over the internet and in the newspaper. At the same time, what he says gives me a glimmer of hope.

"Now, unless you have any more questions, I've got work to do." Lieutenant Sumpter looks right at me while he waits for me to respond.

For a moment, I'm not quite sure what to say, but then I give him a nod. "We're fine, thanks."

Lilah, Jeremy, and I sit in silence while he lets himself out of the house. Even though I have a lot to say, I can't seem to form any words, and it's Jeremy who speaks first.

"I'm going to leave you two alone," he says, giving me a smile. "I think that the two of you have a lot to talk about."

I have to force myself to stand and walk over to him. When I do, he shakes my hand, giving me a smile. "You'll be okay," he tells me. "I promise. This is over, Grey, and you and Lilah can finally get back to your lives."

"I know." My voice is tight and he gives me one more smile before leaving. Before I turn to look at Lilah, I lock the door, then slowly turn around. "Well, Lilah?"

She looks better than she did in the hospital, although I

think that she still looks pale. She'd be ticked if I told her that, though, so I haven't mentioned it. Sitting on the sofa with a pillow in her lap, she looks a lot younger than she really is, but still so like her mother.

"I think I'd like pizza," she tells me. "From Giovanni's. What do you say?"

Right now I'm pretty sure that I'd give her anything she wanted, so I nod. "Anything you like," I tell her. "I'm buying."

*R*ead on for the first chapter of The Liar House, available now on Amazon!

I know that I shouldn't have opened my husband's mail. That's something that tends to really drive him nuts. But the elegant, handwritten envelope caught my eye when I was separating the bills from the junk mail this afternoon and I couldn't help but slip my finger under the flap and carefully coax it open.

Thick and creamy, the paper felt good in my hand. At first, I assumed that it had to be a wedding invitation. Nobody spends that kind of money on stationery for a regular letter anymore. The handwriting on the front was smooth and even, not exactly calligraphy, but measured enough that I knew this letter didn't come from someone in a hurry.

My curiosity grew as I pulled the letter from the envelope and slowly turned it over in my hands so that I could really examine it. And the further I read, the more excited I became.

It was just what my husband and I needed—a little getaway together so that we could connect and really grow our relationship. That's what my therapist told me that we needed, anyway. Grant had always refused to go with me. And now we had this perfect excuse to get out of town.

Trembling, I slipped the invitation back into the envelope and set it by his plate on the table. After he had a whiskey and got something to eat then I was sure that he'd be thrilled to see what the invitation said. There was no way that he would want to pass up this opportunity.

~

"Absolutely not."

Grant puts the letter down carefully on the table, his eyes locked on mine as he speaks. His jaw is tight, which it only ever is when he's really serious about something. I've seen this exact same expression on his face before, when dealing with late-night phone calls from his job.

Even so, I search his face for the joke. He has to be kidding. I'm not even sure that he read the invitation all the way through before declaring that it wasn't an option. I open my mouth to speak, but he cuts me off.

"Susan," he says, his voice kinder this time, "you know as well as I do that the house would simply fall apart without you here to take care of everything. Can you imagine the mess that we'd come home to?" He shakes his head like he's talking to a child. "It would take you *days* to get back on top of it all."

"But how would there be a mess if we weren't here to make it?" He's probably right, but I can't wrap my mind around his logic. "I mean, if we're not here," I continue, speaking faster. "If we're not here to make a mess then there won't be one for me to clean up when we get home."

He knows that. Maybe he's just automatically remembering back to when the kids were still here, but things are different now that they've both flown the coop. Maggie went first, moving all the way across the country to study in California, and Bennett left two years later, going to Maine. Their college choices prove that they couldn't be more different. I still love both of my children and my heart aches that they're not here anymore. Some days, and I know it sounds crazy, I'd give anything to have their mess to clean up again.

At the same time, I have enjoyed having a bit more time to myself, of course I have. It's been nice to finish the chores around the house and then just be able to sit and read some. I'd never let Grant know that I have so much down time in the afternoons, though. I'm sure that he'd come up with something else for me to do to fill my time.

"Susan." There's an edge that has come into his voice when he says my name that lets me know that he's not willing to talk about this any longer. "You know that a mess always happens. I'm simply trying to protect you from having too much work to do when we get back home."

Heat flames in my cheeks. Grant has always looked out for me. When we had trouble getting pregnant, he was more than willing to work longer hours to pay for the treatment. Now that both of the kids are gone, he's let me have two nights a week all to myself, telling me that there's always more work he can catch up with at the office.

I wish that he were here with me more often, especially on the weekends, but I also know that being a top drug rep keeps you on the road for long hours. It's not his fault that he's so good at his job, and that it requires him to travel so much.

I'm disappointed. I really need this break. We've been

friends with Frank and Rosemary for decades, and they've been trying for years to get the two of us to come spend some time with them at their beautiful lake house. The invites are usually extended over calls or texts, so the fact that this one came in a fancy-dancy envelope tells me that Rosemary means business this time.

"You've always protected me, and I appreciate it," I tell him, reaching across the table to take his hand. His skin is warm and smooth in mine and I rub my thumb against his. "My entire adult life I've known that you've always had my back, Grant. But you work too hard. I want you home in the evenings more often, and I want to take this trip with you."

Surely he'll see that I want this for the two of us, together, not just for me. There's no ulterior motive, no specific reason that I want to leave the house with him other than the fact that I just want to spend some quality time with my husband.

Spending some time at the lake house sounds nice too, although that's definitely a secondary reason to go. I know that he's never liked lake houses as much as I do, but that's my dream life, so even living it vicariously through Rosemary for the weekend is sure to make me happy.

I'm getting under his skin, I can tell. Grant has never had a good poker face, which is one reason it's probably just as well that he didn't become a lawyer. Not to mention him being around all of the young, attractive assistants. He's just as dashing as he was when we got married twenty-five years ago. And me, well, I've aged, I'll admit it.

I still remember the way he'd dropped down onto one knee one day when I'd just gotten home from my job at the bank. My feet were screaming from standing all day counting back bills for people who had more money than I could ever hope to have. It was supposed to be a job with plenty of upward mobility, but in the small town where we lived, the reality was that female tellers were only ever going to be just that. Female tellers.

My aching feet were all I could think about when I got out of my car, but then I'd seen Grant sitting on my front porch. As I got closer, he got down onto his knee and pulled out a ring, asking me to marry him.

At first, I wasn't sure. I loved Grant, I really did, but there had always been a tiny part of me whispering in the back of my mind, wondering if I could do better, if there was some way that I could find a man who would give me more. I think that Grant guessed that, even though I'd never have said anything, of course. I didn't want to hurt him, but I wanted to be sure that I didn't settle.

"I promise you," he'd said to me, holding the ring up between the two of us, "that I'll work hard to give you whatever it is that you want. You'll have it all, Susan, no matter what. Kids. A white picket fence. A career. Anything, I don't care, as long as the two of us are together for the rest of our lives. I want to build a family with you, Susan, and I'm willing to share everything that I have with you."

"You'll give me everything?" I had asked him, my voice breathless at the thought. Even though I wasn't sure what I wanted from him, I need to hear from his lips that he was really willing to give me anything that I wanted.

"Anything and everything." The ring caught the light from my front porch and winked at me. It was too small, I remember thinking with a twinge of disappointment, but I knew that I could get a bigger one from him one day. That would be his first way to prove to me that he was serious about what he was saying.

"Anything and everything," I agreed, pulling him up to

me to kiss him. He slipped the ring on my finger—it was a perfect fit—and we set the date that night.

Could I have done better? Maybe. Maybe not. I glance down at the ring on my finger, long since upgraded to something bigger and better. Grant's made good on his promise up until now. He proved to me that he was willing to build the life I wanted when he dropped out of law school simply because I asked him to. It was thanks to him that I even got the job at the bank in the first place. If he hadn't known the person who was hiring, I probably wouldn't have been considered, not with so many other qualified applicants.

I owe him everything, but right now I just want this one thing from him, and for the first time, he's refusing.

Anger coils in me as I stare at him. He's kept his good looks, his strong jaw, he hasn't run to fat. While most other men his age dye their hair, his is still thick and almost black, with only a few flecks of gray appearing around his ears.

"Grant." I let out a sigh. There are few things in the world that I hate more than arguing, but this is something that I really, really want. "Grant, I need this. You promised me anything and everything, do you remember that?"

He nods. "Yes, I do, but I just don't think that it's a good idea, Susan. You'll be overwhelmed when we get back here and you know that I've never wanted a lake house." How he can keep his voice so measured and soft when I'm getting so frustrated is beyond me, but I do my best to match his tone and keep the anger from my voice.

"We're not buying a lake house," I tell him. "We're taking a vacation with our best friends at *their* lake house. Come on, Grant, you know I've always wanted to live on a lake. Please."

"And you know that I've always done what's best for you, no matter if you could see it at the time or not." He paused, looked at me for a second. "This isn't just about the vacation, is it?"

It's not, but I'm not going to tell him that right now. Yes, some of this is about getting to see our best friends, but really, there's more. I've always thought that living on a lake would allow me to be my happiest and best self, and Grant has never given that to me. I want to have that, even if only for a short time.

"Really think about what it is that you want," I tell him, slowly standing up. Dinner was delicious, trout with roasted veggies, but the meal is sitting heavily in my stomach. "I know that you don't think this is a good idea, but think about it, Grant. Please. For me."

With that, I turn and stalk back into the kitchen. There's an opened bottle of wine on the counter and I pour myself a glass, hopeful that just one will be more than enough to calm my nerves and keep me from feeling like I'm going out of my skin while I wait for his response.

Keep reading for free here>>